Bolan takes  and washes

The Executioner stood at the controls of a water cannon, hitting the enemy with a high-pressure blast.

And it was working—in the darkness of night, the heavy stream pummeled down on the ship, cleansing it of terrorists.

Bolan believed, for one short moment, that he had the bastards beat.

But the terrorists had already emptied massive amounts of crude oil onto the ocean's surface. Now they put a torch to it.

The night lit up. The sea was set ablaze. And Mack Bolan felt the weight of crushing defeat....

Also available from Gold Eagle Books,
publishers of the Executioner series:

Mack Bolan's
ABLE TEAM

#1 Tower of Terror
#2 The Hostaged Island
#3 Texas Showdown
#4 Amazon Slaughter
#5 Cairo Countdown
#6 Warlord of Azatlan
#7 Justice by Fire
#8 Army of Devils

Mack Bolan's
PHOENIX FORCE

#1 Argentine Deadline
#2 Guerilla Games
#3 Atlantic Scramble
#4 Tigers of Justice
#5 The Fury Bombs
#6 White Hell
#7 Dragon's Kill
#8 Aswan Hellbox

MACK BOLAN

THE EXECUTIONER 59

BOLAN

Crude Kill

A GOLD EAGLE BOOK FROM

WORLDWIDE

TORONTO • NEW YORK • LONDON • PARIS
AMSTERDAM • STOCKHOLM • HAMBURG
ATHENS • MILAN • TOKYO • SYDNEY

First edition November 1983

ISBN 0-373-61059-9

Special thanks and acknowledgment to
Chet Cunningham for his contributions to this work.

Printed in Canada

"Keep ye the law—be swift in all obedience.
Clear the land of evil, drive the road and
bridge the ford. Make ye sure to each his own,
That he reap where he hath sown.... "
                                    —*Rudyard Kipling*

"A man that studieth revenge
keeps his own wounds green. "
                                    —*Francis Bacon*

"Revenge is fruitless. Revenge is hollow,
offering petty change to the victor—and even
the change is plastic, worthless. To clear the
world of evil itself is the ultimate task, the only
fitting path for men such as myself. "
                                    —*Mack Bolan*

In memory of Robert Clayton Ames,
Middle East analyst, killed in the terrorist
bomb blast that demolished part of the
U.S. Embassy in Beirut on April 18, 1983.

1

The eyes of a furious zealot tracked Mack Bolan as he slipped silently into the darkened Milan residence courtyard. The man stared along his pistol sight, his finger curved around a blued trigger, and squeezed smoothly.

The Executioner's keen night vision helped him catch the slight movement in the shadows of the first doorway ahead. He jolted to one side, dropping low into the deeper blackness just as the night exploded with three shots. Muzzle-flashes pinpointed the gunman in the entranceway. The nightfighter had swung up his silenced Beretta 93-R machine pistol as he dropped. It coughed three times, the suppressor choking down the blast of steel-jacketed 9mm death messengers. All three tore into the ambusher's head, slamming him backward against the wall already splattered with the gunman's hot blood and brain tissue.

Before the body slumped to the dusty entrance, Bolan was running alongside the house. A light blinked on at his left but died at once. He kicked open a door and moved into the room, the Beretta in his right hand scanning the space from end to end. Two candles flickered on a small table. The room was empty.

Ahead he saw a doorway covered by a beaded curtain. Beyond was a hallway. Bolan ran toward it.

The Executioner carried weapons for a hard hit on this rattlesnake's nest. On his right hip hung the unstoppable .44 AutoMag he called Big Thunder. Under his left arm rested the Beretta 93-R. Hardpunching C-4 plastique, detonators and special surprises nestled in pockets hung from his combat webbing. Three U.S. Army fragmentation grenades rode on the straps as well as one Willy Peter white phosphorous grenade, two knives and various ammo pouches.

Ahead of the nightscorcher, a man wearing white pants without a shirt jumped from a doorway into the hall, spilling light around him. He swung a long gun toward Bolan. The Beretta chugged once and the guy thundered into permanent retirement, a hole blossoming in his heart. The sound of retreating footsteps came from the courtyard.

The Executioner kicked open the next door down the hall and stormed inside. The room was empty. Around a corner to the left were three more doors. The first room was vacant. In the second he noticed someone had been sleeping but had obviously left quickly.

Bolan heard a groan.

The sound came from the third room. The door was locked. He concentrated his weight behind his boot and slammed it against the door. The casing inside splintered and the panel burst open. In the dim light the Executioner saw a man lying on a bed, reaching with a wavering hand for a military .45 automatic beside him.

Bolan's Beretta centered on the form. His trigger finger tightened, then eased off. He saw that the man was critically wounded and did not have the strength to lift or aim the weapon.

"No," Bolan commanded. The man halted in his wounded haze. Bolan turned and ran back to the end of the hall where he found a set of steps slanting upward. A figure appeared at the landing above and blasted two shots at Bolan, then vanished as the Executioner sent three rounds chasing him. As Bolan rushed up the steps he rammed a fresh 20-round magazine in the 93-R and peered over the landing from shoe-top level. Ten feet away a small man holding a grenade stared back.

Angling his Beretta upward, the Executioner blasted off a burst, stitching a three-dot message across the guy's face. The man still held the grenade, but his lifeless body fell, fingers relaxed, and the grenade rolled free. As it turned, the thin metal safety spoon flipped off and clattered on the wooden floor.

Bolan swung away, moved like lightning, then hit the floorboards.

Four-point-two seconds later a blast shook the building. Instantly Bolan surged up and ran toward the explosion. Now the game was search and destroy. House-to-house combat, the Army way: clear each room as you moved forward. The next room was empty. Nothing stirred in the house. But there were more terrorists here, Bolan knew. He could feel them.

A woman's wail sounded down the hall. Bolan stopped. He moved through another empty room and down the hall to a war room. Large-scale maps had been tacked to the wall. A dozen red pushpins identified places around the world.

Yellow pins were pressed in another dozen places. Signs in Italian were taped to the wall. A business-sized desk, littered with papers, sat at the side of the room. On the far wall a closet door jiggled. Bolan put a 3-round burst into the panel, chest high. A muffled scream rose, then faded and died as the door swung open and a middle-aged man fell forward holding his chest. Blood seeped between his fingers and a small automatic pistol. He expired as he fell to the floor.

Bolan searched on. The next room was vacant, then another locked door. One hard kick jolted the door inward and the Executioner stepped into a woman's room.

Two teenaged girls, wearing blouses and blue jeans, sat on a king-size water bed; both were chained to the frame.

"Please help us," one of them pleaded in English.

Bolan instructed them to pull downward and hard on the chains. Big Thunder roared twice and the chains came free from the headboard. He darted to the hallway and looked out.

"How many people live here?" Bolan asked.

"Nine, ten, up to twenty," the same girl answered. "Can you help us escape?"

The Executioner nodded curtly. "Stay right behind me." He saw no one in the hall, cleared two more rooms, then came to a rear stairway. He went down the steps three at a time, met no resistance and waved the girls out a back door into the night.

A heavy handgun roared from the corridor behind Bolan and plaster showered on him from the wall. He turned the 93-R, spraying six rounds down the hall. He saw a foot vanish into the next ground-floor room. Bolan moved silently down the hall and peered into the room from a crouch.

It was an armory. Dozens of rifles rested in racks. Boxes of ammunition were stacked high against the walls. Combat gear of all types lay on shelves. He spotted a pair of rocket launchers and boxes of rounds. Bolan waited. Two minutes later he heard someone clear his throat deep inside the room. Then a boot scraped across the wooden floor. The Executioner calculated where the terrorist was—behind the first row of wooden boxes halfway down the room. The nightfighter lifted his Beretta machine pistol, sighted over the top of the boxes and waited. A minute later he saw black hair rise over the box top, then an inch of forehead. The man stopped a moment, and Bolan refined his sight. A fraction of a second later the head pushed up to eye level. Bolan fired. Three kisses of death drilled through the terrorist's forehead, slamming him into a stack of army blankets on his way to eternity.

The Executioner cleared the armory. There were enough weapons and gear there to outfit a platoon of infantry. He put a blob of C-4 plastique on a carton of hand grenades, inserted a pencil detonator-timer and set it for ten minutes. He looked at his watch, then activated the timer.

As he moved into the hallway, a 6-round burst of hot lead splashed into the wall beside him. Bolan dived back through the open door. The fire had come from the room at the end of the corridor.

He pushed the Beretta around the doorframe and sent six rounds into the far room. Three shots replied, one chipping the wooden frame over him. The Executioner jerked an Army frag grenade from his webbing, pulled out the safety pin, permitted the metal arming spoon to pop off and let the bomb ''cook'' for two seconds before he threw it into the room. The four seconds were spent by the time the grenade landed. It went off with a dust-billowing roar.

The big guy was less than two seconds behind it, charging down the hall, chattering off 3-round bursts from the 93-R in a routine assault-fire pattern.

Just before he entered the room, Bolan pulled the big .44. There was no need for the minicannon. The grenade had riddled the room that had once been a work area. The lifeless body of a young man in pajama bottoms had been flung over a small table by the blast that also shredded his face, escorting him into hell.

Bolan left, cleared the last ground-floor room, then trotted back to the wounded man in the bed.

The guy had not moved. He could not move.

The Executioner pushed the .45 away from the weak hand and watched the Italian terrorist. He was about forty, weathered, alert, with a festering bullet hole, taken in an earlier terrorist gunfight, just below his heart. It was amazing that the man was alive.

"I speak some English," the Italian said slowly, prepared to barter for his life.

"Where is Lutfi?" Bolan demanded, his cold eyes boring into their target.

The wounded man shook his head.

Bolan took his face in both hands and stared hard at the wounded man who shivered as he looked at sudden death in the eyes of the black-suited one-man army.

"Ten seconds," the Executioner said softly. "Tell me where Lutfi is in ten seconds or you'll join your buddies."

The terrorist on the bed swallowed, his glance sped to the door, then back to the intensely frigid, unreadable eyes.

"Lutfi was here. He got out when the first shot came. He's going to London."

"Where in London? Tell me and you live. I'll get you a doctor."

The terrorist muttered an address in London, and another in Paris where Lutfi often stayed. Bolan memorized both. Time was falling away quickly now. He had only two minutes to get out of the house before it blew. Bolan looked around the room. It was part sickroom, part office. Near the bed lay a dozen sheets of an Italian newspaper. In a drawer he found a Largo-Star submachine gun with a full clip. Bolan slung it over his shoulder.

A stack of newspapers on the desk caught his attention. Several papers had items circled with a wide-tipped red marking pen. He leafed through them. Halfway down he found an English-language edi-

tion. The page was anchored by a picture of a huge
tanker. The tanker was not circled in red, but it
caught Bolan's attention because of its size. He read
the article below the photo:

> The *Contessa* completed her maiden voyage this
> week, discharging the last of more than 1.5
> million tons of crude oil into waiting tanks,
> pipelines and smaller tankers in six different
> countries in Europe. She will be making regular
> runs from the Persian Gulf. The *Contessa* is
> nearly a half mile long and 435 feet wide. She
> cost the American owners over two hundred for-
> ty million dollars to build.

Bolan checked the circled pictures in the other
papers more closely and noted that they included
various individuals, banks, famous buildings, even
one museum. Four of the photos circled were of the
Prince of Wales. Everything marked could be a potential victim of a kidnapping, or a hijack target for a
terrorist.

The nightfighter checked the rest of the desk. In a
lower drawer he found samples of bomb fuses that
had been waterproofed. He also discovered a complete miniaturized radio transmitter that could work
as a trigger and a small receiver that could act as the
receiver-detonator. To his surprise, both had also
been waterproofed. They were well made, up to the
state of the art. It looked like Lutfi was ready to do
any job.

The Executioner glanced back at the wounded

man. He was in pain. The recent gunfire would soon bring the Italian police. The warrior picked up the wounded terrorist. The searing pain caused the guy to pass out. Twenty seconds later Bolan carried the man out the back gate of the house into the neighboring yard. He laid the unconscious man near the rear door of the house and walked toward the next street.

Before he had gone fifty yards, Lutfi's two-story headquarters shattered into rubble as a giant explosive fist tore it apart. A dozen smaller explosions penetrated the hushed Milan sky, then flames leaped from the wreckage. In the distance the sirens of approaching police cars sounded.

The lawmen would soon find the wounded man and he would be treated: a bargain kept.

Bolan hurried toward his rented car. Jack Grimaldi would be waiting, anxious to be moving.

Bolan had jetted out of Stony Man Farm to get to Milan that morning, even before all the details of his mission were spelled out. His immediate job was to find and terminate Lutfi, a terrorist, the most hated international criminal currently in action. Lutfi was a serious overmatch for any small nation, and Lutfi always had the advantage of a surprise attack. He was ingenious, fearless and absolutely amoral. And he could pick his time and place.

So the Executioner had started his own personal campaign against Lutfi.

He would use the man's own tactics and fight force with force. He would fight with a deadly, efficient weapon called *The Bolan Effect*.

It was an effect that found its own enemies. Bolan's methods could intercept an individual's dark destiny of death and turn it back on itself long before any back-up agency or force could locate the menace for him. It was almost as if terror—human horror in all its forms—became magnetized toward the night-fighter and forced his hand.

Because of this, Bolan could act before any front-line fighters could. Indeed, Bolan already acted before the intelligence bureaucracies did. He acted before the armed services brass did. He acted before any single part of the chain of command could act, however impressive the total organization might be. And often, Bolan acted before the enemy did.

In this case, Lutfi had escaped death and thereby won the first battle.

But not the war.

Not the war that Bolan, personally, had just declared.

2

The Executioner sat in a plush office at American International Imports of Rome, a cover operation for his latest, post-Congo activities in the Italian capital. It was a little after midnight. Bolan stretched out his long legs and looked at the standard heavy-scrambler attachment he had fitted on the telephone handset.

The conference call to Stony Man Farm was soon in confusion.

"Hold it," Bolan commanded softly into the phone. "I can hear only one of you at a time." He paused and the line remained silent. "Is there anything new on Lutfi?"

April Rose's soft, efficient voice responded quickly.

"We do have a positive ID on your man, Mack. Now we know for sure he was the assassin who wounded Walt Harrison two weeks ago and killed his two security men. Oh—" She stopped suddenly.

For a second, only April Rose's sharp intake of breath sounded over the wire. Then Hal Brognola's steady voice filled the void.

"I'm sorry, Striker. We didn't know about it until this afternoon. Harrison died about an hour ago. They tried everything they could."

Mack Bolan gripped the receiver tighter and closed his eyes. A bitter taste surged into his mouth. He swallowed several times.

"Yeah. Okay. We...we expected it. He was just hit too bad, too often."

"We're all sorry, Striker. I know you two were longtime friends." Brognola paused for a moment and the line hummed, softly, respectfully silent.

Brognola broke the quiet. "Striker, it's far past time that this madman Lutfi was brought to justice. You have all possible latitude. Our intel shows the mission is still as hard as they come: search and destroy. Find Lutfi."

Bolan took a second deep breath. His brain was whirling. He heard all that Brognola said, but he was still weathering the shock. Walt, damn. He had been a fine soldier. Yeah, and he would be missed. The Executioner had been in Nam with the big redhead. They had worked many missions side by side in the days of Able. Then the guy took a field commission, was wounded and shipped stateside. The day Walt received his Army discharge, he joined the State Department. The man had become a popular and outstanding politician. Later he had secretly renewed his friendship with Mack Bolan during Bolan's incarnation as Colonel John Phoenix, to become one of the few men in Washington that Bolan could personally relate to. Bolan liked him for his directness, his energy, his ability to get things done. He was not a pencil pusher, he was a man of action. Right up to his death.

Bolan jerked his attention back to the phone.

Kurtzman was talking. "We'll telemeter anything else we can get on Lutfi to your Rome office. You'll have everything I dig up. It'll be there in the morning. This is a guy who likes to function on his own most of the time, Mack."

"Send it all to London, instead," Bolan said. He gave them a quick recap of his firefight in Milan.

"I saw a picture of a ship, the *Contessa*, one of those huge oil tankers. Does the name mean anything to anyone?"

Brognola responded. "I remember something about her. Biggest tanker in the world. Cost nearly a quarter of a billion dollars to build. Do you think she ties into the Lutfi mission?"

"Probably not. Nothing points that way. The picture was in a British newspaper in Lutfi's Milan headquarters. It was just one shot among a lot of them. The others had people and firms circled in red ink. The circles could mark a group of potential targets for Lutfi. On this one we cover all the angles." He paused. "Why don't you dig up anything you can find about the ship and send it along to London."

"You got it, Colonel," Kurtzman said.

"The problem is going to be finding Lutfi," Bolan said. "I've got two addresses to check out, but I don't have much hope. If I knew his next target, his next operation, we'd have something firm. It all depends on the situation and terrain, as my old sergeant used to say in Germany." Bolan paused briefly. "Jack and I'll be taking off in the Cat for London tonight. Anything else for me?"

"All clear here with me," Brognola said.

"I'm getting to work," Kurtzman said, signing off.

"Boss Lady?"

"Yes, Mack," April Rose said in her business-efficient voice. "Everything is geared up to assist. You'll have all the input we can find by morning. I'm sure you can obtain any tools of the trade you'll need."

"True."

The line was silent for a few seconds.

"The others are off the line," she said. Another pause. "I still don't like goodbyes, Mack."

"This isn't a goodbye, Lady. I'll be back." But a sudden uneasiness had crept into his inflection, a huskiness into his voice.

"You better be, Mack. We had that picnic all planned, the sandwiches made."

The line was silent.

"We'll have that picnic. We'll have sand and ants and maybe a rain shower, don't worry." There was a pause. "I have to go now."

"Yes. I know that. Go, Striker. Please be careful."

"Roger, Lady. Careful."

The Executioner heard the connection break and put the big handpiece back on the cradle.

A half hour later Mack Bolan and Jack Grimaldi took off from Rome in a U.S. Air Force F-14 Tomcat. Somewhere high over Paris the bird gulped down a large drink of jet fuel from a USAF flying tanker. The nozzle came away, Bolan waved at the 20,000 foot-high filling-station crew and the Tomcat streaked on toward London, cruising at just over 600 miles per hour.

Before daylight, Grimaldi dropped the jet into a top-security military air base near London. Within an hour both men were bedded down in bunks. As they slept, the Tomcat was serviced, inspected, fueled and put in top shape ready for another trip at a moment's notice.

COLONEL JOHN PHOENIX left the BOQ just after ten that morning wearing English-cut slacks, a brown jacket and a tie. The jacket was a loose fit, hiding the Executioner's professional tools.

He caught a cab into the city. En route he changed taxis twice, making sure no one followed him, and then took a third to the address provided by the wounded terrorist in Milan.

The small retail shop looked particularly unproductive. The name over the windowed door read: Resonor's, Gentlemen's Apparel.

The moment Bolan entered the shop he felt unseen eyes evaluating him, the same way he had felt on that sour recon patrol in Nam a few seconds before the Charlies opened up on his squad.

The nightfighter turned and received sudden smiles from a pair of frumpy, sixtyish shopowners. The men were short, ruddy complexioned, gray haired and smoked identical briar pipes. One man stood, grumbled and came forward with a sprightly walk. He studied Bolan a moment and nodded.

"Aye, guv'nor. What might I help you with this morning?"

"Looking, just looking," Bolan announced.

The shop owner frowned.

"Well, actually I'm interested in a good tweed jacket, if it isn't too expensive."

"Young man, in good clothing quality never comes cheap. This way, please. I have some interesting jackets to show you."

Bolan followed the man toward the rear of the shop and, for the next five minutes, pretended to be interested in tweed jackets. At the same time, he reconned the place. Nothing suspicious, no weapons showing, no hardcases lurking.

The small Englishman showed the Executioner a tweed suit, which he said was the finest in all of London. The price was three hundred pounds. Bolan shook his head.

"Too much for me," Bolan said. Suddenly, without any obvious cause, he again felt danger with his sixth sense. There were spying eyes trained on the back of his neck.

The Executioner turned quickly, staring behind him.

Nothing.

A door closed softly, nearby.

"I'll browse around for a while," Bolan said, moving slowly toward the sound of the door. He found only more displays of suits and counters of accessories. Then the aisle dead-ended at a wooden panel. The shopkeeper trailed him, talking constantly.

"Perhaps something in a Donegal with a hint of

green in the pattern? Tweeds are going to be the style this coming season.''

There was something different about the wall ahead of the nightfighter. It was plain, but it was unusual, like a stage setting. Then he saw the hint of a door outlined in the wood-grained vertical pattern. A concealed door.

Bolan took three quick steps and hurled his bulk at the wall, jumping at the last second and slamming both boots against the wood three feet off the floor. A two foot wide vertical section of the wall propped inward, ripping screws from wood, shredding a concealed doorjamb, splintering the veneer.

Behind Bolan the small man screeched in protest. The Executioner's force carried him into the hidden adjoining room. The room was small, with a table, typewriter, stacks of newspapers, books and a World War II-type hand grenade lying on the papers. Just beyond, a flight of steps led upward.

Bolan grabbed the grenade, made sure the safety pin was in place and dashed up the steps three at a time. His 93-R Beretta was too big to carry comfortably under the sport jacket, but on the lanyard there was room enough. He pulled the Beretta from inside his coat as he charged up the steps. At the top he found a room full of workbenches. Spread on one bench was a layout of quarter-pound rectangles of C-4 plastique explosive, sophisticated radio timer-detonators, cardboard boxes, packing, wires, small antenna and, strangely enough, an assortment of fancy birthday-gift wrappings. It was a bomb factory.

A door opposite him burst open and a man charged through with a pistol belching angry lead. The Beretta sneezed twice, and the charging man's nose disintegrated as the burrowing 9mm slugs cut upward into his brain, pulping half a dozen vital activity centers, dumping the lifeless hulk against the wall where it slid slowly to the floor.

Behind the first man a second materialized, holding a submachine gun. The guy's trigger finger was tightening when Bolan's 93-R wheezed. The shots slapped through the terrorist's neck. Blood vomited onto the wood floor in a growing pool where he fell. The dark stain grew until the man's heart stopped pumping.

Movement sounded in the corridor out the far door. The Executioner ran to the door, squatted and peered around the jamb: he saw a hallway with two doors.

He fisted his .44 AutoMag and took a cautious step into the hall. Before he could draw a second breath, a blur of an army-fatigue-clad figure surged from a door fifteen feet ahead of him with a chatter gun firing on full automatic. Melting lead burned past Bolan's shoulder. Even with his speed it took a fraction of a beat to lift Big Thunder and fire twin demons of death at the figure.

Bolan heard the double roar of the minicannon in the narrow hallway and saw both rounds hit home.

The Executioner's head ached from the sound of the booming firefight in the confined space. Then suddenly it was graveyard quiet. Rapidly he checked both rooms; they were empty. He bent over the figure wearing fatigues. As Bolan rolled the corpse over, long blond hair tumbled from a green army cap. No Italian woman terrorist, this one, not with her soft blue eyes and English bone-china complexion.

She could not have been more than seventeen.

Bolan cursed softly as he ran to the end of the hallway. A terrorist was a terrorist, no matter what sex, age or national origin. They all had the same right to believe what they wanted to, but when they met the Executioner they also had the right to die.

The hallway was empty. He turned into the closest room, which he had already checked. It was a storage area, a supply room for bombs, detonators, fuses, tape, timers, packaging of all kinds, electronic parts and more C-4.

The next room was rigged as a barracks with bunks four high, a jumble of clothing and an alarm clock. He ran back to the bomb-assembly room and looked at the markings on the plastique: British made, but with Italian words. Bolan pushed two of the cubes of death into his pocket and opened a cupboard. Two pages of the *London Times* lay there, both marked in red. One had a circled picture of the changing of the guard at Buckingham Palace. The second had red marker-pen lines around a story about a rich industrialist and his hideaway mansion in the Lake District, and a picture of Prince Charles double circled.

On the lower half of the page from the *Times* was a picture of a ship, the *Contessa*. Bolan stopped. It was the same tanker he had seen in the paper in Milan. In both cases the ship was not circled. Why did it stop him? Coincidence? The Executioner had long since learned there is no such thing as coincidence. A soldier had to believe that and act on it if he wanted to stay alive for long. He folded the sheet of newspaper and put it in his pocket.

If Lutfi was lining up a new target, planning a new operation, the chances were that the circled newspaper items held the key.

He continued his quick search of the cupboard and found a copy of the Paris Daily Ship Sailing Log. It reported daily on every major French port, printing the name of ships that had docked and had cleared. Ships again.

On the bottom shelf he found a recognizable item: a magnetic Limpet mine to attach to a ship. This one was rigged with a directional charge of C-4 plastique—a hull-splitting weapon. Ships once again.

A door slammed somewhere below and Bolan knew it was over. Downstairs in the store, he saw that the English pair had gone and that the outside door stood open as if the shop had been abandoned in haste.

The Executioner, too, left the store. He was a block away before he heard the sirens of the approaching police cars.

LATER, AT THE COMPANY'S LONDON OFFICE, The Executioner checked in and listened to a briefing from a CIA agent he had never met before. The man's name was Perkins, and he seemed to be in charge of more than just the London operation. He was tall, thin, sharp, quick, friendly and helpful.

"The Yard tells us the bomb factory you found is a new one," Perkins said. "There is a definite tie-in with the Italian Red Brigades. The Yard thanks you for your assistance. However, they were a bit upset about finding three dead bodies. Two of them were English nationals, and one they think was an Arab. The corpses will be handled without any unfavorable publicity. Auto accidents, most likely." Perkins paused, offered Bolan an English filter tip, and they both lit up.

"The newspaper you brought was very interesting. We're talking with MI-6 about it now. They're shaken by this development. There is, of course, constant security surrounding Prince Charles. Any blatant preparations, any tracking of the Royal Family is a crisis situation for these people."

A clerk knocked, came in and gave Perkins a thick envelope. The agent checked the name on the front and handed it to Bolan.

"Your signals have arrived."

The Executioner opened the envelope and spread out the material on the edge of the CIA man's desk. There were four pictures of Lutfi, all candids, taken with long lenses. Bolan knew the terrorist was six foot two, but in the pictures he looked shorter. He wore a hat and sport clothes. His face was long and narrow, with a sharp nose, wide-set eyes and the shadow of a heavy beard. He had a slight build. None of the international KGB killers he had eliminated so far fit that description. Lutfi was thought to be Italian, Turkish, or even Polish, not Arabic as his name suggested.

Bolan put aside the typed material on Lutfi and found the six sheets of data on the supertanker. He flipped a picture of the ship to the agent.

"Yes, the *Contessa*," Perkins said. "I've heard of her."

Bolan nodded, suddenly restless in the office. He gathered the material and stuffed it back in the envelope. He would digest it later.

"Normally I work alone," Bolan told Perkins. "But on this one I may need support." Bolan looked at the picture of the supertanker and pushed it in the envelope. "My job now is tracking Lutfi. I want anything you hear about him. If he sneezes, drops his socks or burps, you tell me about it." He nodded to Perkins and left the office.

The Executioner felt strange as he stepped into the London street. He was having a weird series of hunches that did not seem to make sense.

No platoon leader in his right mind would go into combat with the intel Bolan now had on this mission. His only remaining lead was an address in Paris, given to him by a wounded terrorist half out of his mind with pain. But Bolan knew he had to check it out.

The Tomcat would be ready; Grimaldi was always ready. Something ticked away in the back of Bolan's brain, but it would not come to the surface. Nothing seemed to fit. He had to work it out. Lutfi was there, but the victim was in shadows.

He had to beat back the mists and the darkness. It would not be easy, but he had to do it.

3

The northern Italian sky, with a million white-hot holes burned into it, twinkled in the far reaches of hyperspace and relative time. Two Italian jet interceptors whistled off a runway to the east. Lutfi nodded as he lay on the ground, twenty yards from a four-foot-high, eight-foot-wide, double-apron combat fence that the Italians had erected around the far end of their airfield. He smiled at how easy it would be. His spies had told him there was no electronic warning system around the airfield.

Lutfi turned his head, watching the six men crawl up to his heels and wait. He had trained them in the mountains for three days for this strike. All would perform brilliantly, since Lutfi himself had hand-picked the men from twenty volunteers. All would gladly die before failing this mission.

Lutfi was not a leader who sent in men where he would not go himself. The success of this strike depended on penetration and rapid neutralization. Lutfi would lead the attack.

He waved the squad forward. The men stayed low, moving on elbows and toes. At the fence, Lutfi snipped a path through the lowest strands with a pair of wire cutters. He squirmed on his back under the barbed wire, cutting his way, pushing the wire upward and to the side to form a small tunnel. Moments later he was inside the Italian air force field. He waited for his men to go under the fence. Then they stood, formed what Americans called a "column of ducks," and jogged at a seven-minute-per-mile pace through the darkness.

After covering a mile toward the security lights to the south, the men moved into a sandy ditch, lay down and waited.

Lutfi checked his digital watch. Eleven minutes to spare—he had allowed ten minutes for holdups, but they had found no problems so far.

When his watch reached four minutes after midnight, Lutfi formed his unit and marched openly toward a series of low mounds of dirt and sand three hundred yards to the right. All his men wore regular Italian military-fatigue uniforms. Lutfi wore the rank of captain. He swung the six men to a halt in front of a four-foot-square sentry box outside the first dirt-covered concrete bunker.

Lutfi moved quickly to the guard post and returned a salute.

"Captain Lutfi to relieve you of that special shipment of plastic explosives," he said.

The guard frowned. "Sir. I have no written authorization for any material transfer." The soldier choked his objection when he saw Lutfi lift a silenced pistol. The terrorist fired twice and only a soft cough came from the silencer. Both 9mm parabellum rounds from the Mauser Parabellum Swiss pistol tore through the guard's temple, ripping off half his skull, dumping him to the floor of the guard shack.

Two more Italian guards walked around the side of the bunker. They came from where Lutfi knew they would. He cut them down with four shots from the chugging Mauser. That was the last of the guard force.

The six raiders hurried into action with practiced precision. Two men blasted the locks on the bunker door with a minimum charge of plastique. A third punched up the telephone in the guard shack and reported that nothing unusual was going on. When the heavy steel munitions bunker door swung open, Lutfi ran inside and with his pocket flashlight, made sure the explosives were there on the pallet board. Then he hurried outside the ammo bunker, took a small red box from his pocket and pressed its black button twice.

Moments later his red box gave an answering pair of beeps.

"Go," Lutfi instructed his six-man team.

They ran into the bunker and hurried out carrying the foot-square boxes of C-4 to a spot thirty feet in front of the bunker. One man set up a Cartouche light machine gun on a tripod, aiming it down the hard-surfaced road that led to the main section of the air base. A second man ran up with two cans of belt-fed ammunition, inserted the first round from a belt and charged the weapon.

Three minutes later the *whup-whup-whup* of a helicopter stabbed through the previously silent darkness. Sixty seconds passed before the big bird settled on a landing on the tarmac thirty feet from the bunker and beside the stack of boxes. At once the side doors opened, and two men inside helped as the six on the ground loaded the boxes of explosives.

A minute and twenty-eight seconds later the eighty boxes had been stowed on board the aircraft, while its rotors spun at idle.

Two men ran to the machine gun. A vehicle approached. A few moments later the rig came into range, and the crew launched a sizzling firetrack of tracer rounds at the military jeep. Before any return fire came, the rig spun out of control and tipped over. The Cartouche continued to pour rounds into the exposed undercarriage until the tracers found the petrol tank and the jeep exploded into a fireball.

With the precision of long practice, the machine gunner dismounted his weapon, loaded it on the chopper and jumped in. Lutfi stepped into the helicopter and it lifted off, skimming over the fence, then slanting west, staying less than twenty feet off the green Italian countryside.

Lutfi settled back in the aircraft. It had all gone smoothly. Planning was the key, based on good intelligence reports, and diligent training of top-quality experts. His chance of failure on any mission was extremely low.

The real task lay ahead. In twenty minutes they would be out of Italy, across the coastline and over the Mediterranean. The Italian defenses simply did not have sophisticated enough radar or search planes to find the chopper skimming over the waves at twenty feet. In less than a half hour after leaving Italy, they would make their rendezvous.

Then the next-to-last piece of the plan would be in place. This was a critical path point on his mission diagram. It all continued or stopped, depending on this transfer of the plastique.

Lutfi wiped the grit off his face and accepted a congratulatory bottle of wine from the chopper pilot. The dream was a step closer. It was the biggest fantasy of every terrorist.

It was the *equalizer* factor, but no one had ever yet achieved it.

4

The Tomcat broke through the soup at 28,000 feet, slamming past the last bit of death-gray clouds toward an eye-smarting golden sun. Below them the whipped-cream tops of the churning cloud mass looked solid enough to walk on.

Jack Grimaldi piloted the Tomcat through the cold crystal-pure air at 610 miles per hour, high over the English Channel on a short flight to Paris. The Executioner had moved quickly after his talk at the Company office. Soon they would pass the halfway point, and Grimaldi would switch over to the new NATO Joint Military Radio Command control.

Mack Bolan hunched in the tight rear seat of the Tomcat, mulling over his mission. Seldom had he possessed so little hard intel for a job. Search and destroy. Right now the searching was the hard part. Finding was even tougher. His first task was to tie down the terrorist's new location. The true way to do that was to determine the guy's next target.

The aircraft radio chattered in Bolan's headset, but he only half listened. Grimaldi jolted the Executioner from his thoughts.

"Something's cooking," the pilot said. "NATO Joint Military says we should land in Paris at our earliest opportunity. They have a high-priority land-line telephone call waiting for you that is too sensitive to broadcast.''

"Roger. How long to Paris?''

"Ten minutes,'' Grimaldi answered.

"Kick in the afterburners, Jack.''

BOLAN SAT IN AN OFFICE at base operations in an air-field near Paris. He nodded as he spoke into the handset.

"Yes, I heard you, Perkins. How do you know it was Lutfi?''

"Colonel, it has all the telltale marks of his opera-tion: surprise, military efficiency and timing, the 9mm parabellum rounds, no witnesses, knowing pre-cisely where the plastique was stored. He's made two similar snatches at military bases in Italy with this identical pattern.''

"I'll buy that. But why? A kidnapper doesn't need a ton of C-4. What does a terrorist do with fifteen hundred pounds of one of the most powerful ex-plosives in the world?''

"He blows up something damn big.''

"What, Perkins?''

"I don't know, sir. It could be almost anything, or anyone, from what we know of Lutfi.''

"Thanks, Perkins.'' Bolan hung up and stared at the notes on a yellow ruled pad. "Fifteen hundred pounds of C-4 plastique stolen from an Italian air-field,'' he muttered. "Escape by fast chopper, prob-ably directly over the Mediterranean....''

He looked out the window without seeing anything. Target. Target. Target. What was the terrorist's target? For a moment a flash recall shot across the warrior's mind, then vanished. Slowly it came back until it was sharp and clear. "Waterproof fuses and waterproof radio sender with a sensitive receiver-detonator," Bolan whispered.

He frowned and paced.

Limpet mine, Bolan thought.

He ran for the door as the missing pieces of the jigsaw puzzle began dropping into place. *Shaped charges, limpet mines, pictures of the supertanker.*

Bolan felt an icy shiver rocket up his spine. He knew it. He knew Lutfi's target.

The scum was going to attack the *Contessa*. Bolan did not know why or how or when, but Lutfi was going to attack and try to capture or sink the world's largest carrier of crude oil.

Five minutes later Bolan got through to Perkins on the phone. "Her location?" Bolan barked out the question. "Where is the *Contessa* right now? Do you have that registry that lists ships clearing ports?"

"Yes, sir. I've got a man tracking down the sailing registry. But the *Contessa* may not be listed. She never enters a port, she's far too large. She sits seaward and is off-loaded by floating pipelines or by smaller tankers."

"I'll call you back from the flight line, Perkins. You should know where the *Contessa* is by then. Wherever she is, I want to get under way so I can get on site."

It was fifteen minutes before Bolan and Grimaldi had checked out with the French and Grimaldi was satisfied that the Tomcat was ready. The Executioner got an open line to London and located Perkins.

The CIA man sounded worried. "The *Contessa* is in the Mediterranean heading for her second port of call. That means she still has ninety percent of her cargo, over 1.3 million tons of crude oil in her holds."

"Where is she?"

"Ten miles off the coast of France, approaching Toulon. That's 450 miles southeast of Paris near Marseille."

"Good. We're moving now. That's less than an hour from here. We still have some daylight." The nightfighter hung up without saying goodbye. There was no time now for formalities. He waved at Grimaldi and they ran toward the Tomcat, which was plugged in and fired up.

As the twin-tailed jet clawed its way into the sky, Bolan became convinced that his combat reflex about the *Contessa* was correct. He had been in too many situations where there wasn't a day, an hour or even a minute to think through a problem, working it out logically with firm intel. Instead the decision had to be made in seconds, sometimes in a fraction of a second with men's lives depending on it. In those combat crunches he *knew* the answer, the right answer. Again he felt that intense compressed combat logic. The target had to be the *Contessa*. The red-marked newspapers were nothing but a false lead, Lutfi's way of laughing at whoever found them.

France hurtled by below them at 624 miles per hour. From 20,000 feet, France looked like one large green golf course. Soon the Tomcat's sleek nose dropped, starting the letdown toward the southern coast.

Five minutes later they flashed over the ancient city of Toulon with its modern port facilities and the five distinctive basins. But even this port, which could accommodate the world's largest battleship, would not stretch far enough to hold the length of the *Contessa*.

Grimaldi throttled back to reduce speed and soon they saw the floating island, the huge dark mass of the tanker seaward and slightly south. Bolan had walked across the deck of a 500,000-ton supertanker, but the size of the *Contessa* amazed him.

They dropped to 200 feet and buzzed the ship.

"I don't believe it," Grimaldi said over the intercom. "Nothing that big has any right to float."

Bolan stared. She was half a mile long. The ship was an impossibility. She was also a tanker that could disgorge a million tons of crude oil to foul the entire southern coast of France. . . .

Grimaldi switched to the special frequency to contact the ship.

"Tanker *Contessa*, this is the jet aircraft overheard. Can you read me?"

"Yes, Tomcat, we know your twin tails."

"*Contessa*, have you been contacted concerning your safety?"

"Affirmative, Tomcat."

Bolan used his microphone. "*Contessa*, do you have an arms locker on board?"

"Affirmative."

"Is your captain listening?"

A heavier voice sounded through Bolan's earphones.

"Yes. This is Captain Running, Hans Running."

"Captain. I'd suggest that you break out your arms and put every man on guard on that floating island of yours. We'll fly cover for you as long as our fuel holds out."

There was an awkward silence on the air.

"Tomcat, I'm still confused. What's the problem? No one has told me."

"Captain, we believe an international terrorist is going to try to take over your vessel. He'll use every means he can to get possession of your craft and the 1.3 million tons of crude on board. He wants it so he can threaten to spill it."

"My God, dump it?"

"We have a suspect, Captain, and he *would* dump it. Just take all precautions that you can. Put everyone on watch, and be sure they are armed."

"I never thought I'd see the day. All right, Tomcat. We seem to have little choice. We also have orders from the owners and lessors." There was a long sigh. "We'll put the orders into effect at once."

"We'll be upstairs for a while," Bolan said. "Good luck."

Bolan felt the big bird ease upward. Grimaldi put the Tomcat into a gentle climbing turn as he slowly scratched for altitude, so the jet engine would use less fuel for the same amount of thrust.

Bolan pulled a sheaf of papers from his flight suit and leafed through them. They were specifications on the *Contessa*.

The craft was classified as a Super Ultra large Crude Carrier (SUCC). It carried one and a half million tons of crude oil direct from the Persian Gulf to the hungry refineries spread across Europe. She was 2,400 feet long, just short of half a mile, 430 feet from scupper to scupper and seven stories high. She carried everything she needed for a year at sea for her crew and self-maintenance.

For the crew there was recreation equipment: movies, television, a gymnasium, and video computers and a thousand different video games. She was really a floating hotel, with two saunas, two bars, enough filled food lockers and grocery stores to feed an army for a year, central heating and air conditioning, two dining rooms, double staterooms for the ten officers and thirty crewmen, and a mile-long jogging trail around the deck.

Bolan studied the list of equipment and the scientific specifications. There were enough electronics on board to fly a space shuttle to the moon and back. There were complicated computer-linked instruments, sensors, probes and pumps that all functioned in unison to fill the *Contessa*'s holds to precise levels of crude, and then to empty them in any order needed. The ship had ninety holds all constructed of rupture-proof steel.

Other computer-activated instruments piloted the ship and could hold her on a precise course for days at a time without the touch of a human hand regardless of the weather, tides, winds, currents or changes in engine power, since she was locked on to the stars for her precise foot-by-foot guidance across the vast seas.

Bolan heard Grimaldi talking on the radio, getting clearance to land at the military base at Marseille, which was only forty-two miles along the coast. They were expected. Their cover-time fuel had run low. Grimaldi gave a final farewell to Captain Running on the *Contessa*, steaming along below them at her full-load speed of eighteen knots.

Shortly after, they landed at a French airbase.

A half hour after landing, Bolan sat in a room in "officer country" and continued memorizing the layout of the SUCC *Contessa*. The nightfighter hated waiting, but he took advantage of the few free hours to learn the structure and location of the major centers of the ship. He was sure he'd have practical need for all the information.

The huge deck of the craft had three helicopter landing pads, all near the stern, and all reinforced to accept large fully loaded military choppers. She had all types of radar, frontal-scan equipment and communications antennas, depth sounders and display scopes that pictured the seabed under the hull whether it was 50 feet down or 40,000 feet away. The deck was half covered with a maze of pipes that led to each of the main holds for filling and pumping out the crude.

He studied the layout of the holds. The ninety immense tanks were four abreast in columns twenty-two feet long. Holds were situated crossways to the others at each end. Thirteen strategically situated, computer-determined holds were used as permanent ballast tanks so the craft would remain stable and operable even when emptying her cargo. These ballast holds held 312,000 tons of seawater.

Two of the holds became scavenger tanks, where the cleanings from the sixty-five cargo holds were pumped. This ensured that no oil spills or oil clean-outs could result from swabbing down the empty holds. The scavenger tanks were pumped out with the regular crude, since high-pressure crude was used as the cleaner.

The remaining sixty-five cargo holds could handle a little under 24,000 tons of oil each. Bolan lifted his eyebrows. What an ideal target for a terrorist who wanted international attention and probably a huge ransom, not only for the release of the giant ship but also in exchange for not dumping the oil.

Such an event would happen over Bolan's dead body.

5

The jet helicopter sliced through the blackness of midnight, slanting away from the Italian coastal town of Savona, roving ten miles seaward, then cutting north. It soon turned back over the coast and moved cross-country into the hills behind San Remo. The bird and its cargo were only a few miles from the French border.

Lutfi and his men rested for sixteen hours in a farmhouse hidden in the hills. Then, again in the darkness, they boarded the same chopper. The heavily laden craft angled toward the sea, turned west and followed the French coastline a mile over the water, sliding past Nice, Cannes and St. Tropez. They passed over the Iles D'Hyeres and gained some altitude, coming off the wave tops so the men could search the black water.

"There," Lutfi said softly and the pilot homed in on a single light half a mile north. The craft circled slowly, made certain the ship was the one they wanted, and then the pilot inched the special rubber-encased landing struts down toward the ship's deck.

Lutfi tensed as he watched the delicate process. One slip here and his whole project would sink.

Two minutes later the helicopter had settled solidly on the slightly rolling deck of a surfaced World War

II German U-boat. As soon as the rotors stopped spinning, the torpedo supply hatch opened and two men dressed in dark blue hurried out and lashed the chopper to the open decking and to prepositioned cleats. Then, with military precision, the cases of C-4 plastique were off-loaded into the submarine's forward hatch. All lights had been turned off. The men worked with cool efficiency in the blackness.

Lutfi checked his glowing watch dial and drummed fingers on the edge of the helicopter until the last case was safely lowered inside. At last he motioned his men to enter the U-boat. He talked a moment with the pilot before the two sub crewmen untied the landing struts. Lutfi and the sailors hurried below into the Nazi ship killer and looked out the hatch. Lutfi listened to the chopper's growl as it lifted off the underseas vessel. The sub rose with new buoyancy.

A smiling young man with a full beard met Lutfi.

"My good friend and comrade. Right on time. I knew you would make it." He spoke in Italian.

Lutfi answered in the same language.

"Carlo. Is everything ready? Any problems?"

"All ready, and no problems. We will make a strike that the world will never forget. We will obtain the ultimate weapons. Our glorious cause will prevail now and for a thousand years."

Lutfi held up his hand to stop the stream of Red Brigades party propaganda he knew was coming. He smiled to take some of the sting from the quick action.

"Later, Carlo, later. We have much work to do and little time. It will be daylight in two hours. How far to the target?"

"The *Contessa* is a half hour from us, landward. We have observed her on the skyline and believe she is anchored for unloading tomorrow."

"Perfect, Carlo. You will receive special recognition. Now, show me the details. I want to see our forward-firing tubes. All four are operational as you promised? And did you get your twenty men?"

"Yes, all four tubes will fire, and we have twenty-eight men. As we discussed, our fish can dive to no more than twenty meters, but that should be enough. We shouldn't need to go below periscope depth."

"Which is where we should be right now, Captain. We don't want daylight to catch us surfaced. Take her down."

The young Italian went to the small control room midships and gave the curt orders. After one false start his inexperienced crewmen took the old warrior beneath the waves and leveled her off at periscope depth.

Lutfi smiled.

He was now only one giant step away from his goal—ultimate power.

TWO HOURS AFTER SUNRISE the German U-boat had maneuvered to within half a mile of the tanker *Contessa*. Lutfi lifted his brows when he saw the SUCC through the periscope. He could not believe the size of it. He swung the glass in search of his first target.

For three hours the U-boat waited for a victim. Then at last it came, a small 20,000-ton "ferry" tanker heading for the *Contessa* to begin the job of off-loading 200,000 tons of crude into the port of Toulon and directly into the refinery tanks.

"Your target, Captain," Lutfi said, turning the periscope over to Carlo. The young Italian reversed his cap and draped his arms over the extended silver handles as he turned the tube, following the small tanker.

"Flood all tubes forward," the captain said. "Connect the target-position calculator. Firing will be from the bridge."

The man at the calculator in the conning tower followed the orders.

"Enemy position, starboard bow, angle fifty. Enemy speed, five knots, range, 200 meters. Torpedo speed, thirty. Depth at ten."

Carlo did not have to worry about the proper lead angle for the torpedo; that was the job of the calculator, which was connected directly with the gyrocompass and the TBT column along with the torpedoes. Every change in the boat's course was automatically translated to the torpedoes. Carlo merely had to keep the target in the cross hairs of the glass on the TBT column.

"Connect tubes one and two," Carlo shouted.

The long black cigar of the submersible hung nearly motionless in the emerald green of the Mediterranean.

Then Carlo nodded. "Fire one," he thundered.

The throbbing came through the hull as the compressed air slammed the torpedo out of its tube. The U-boat lifted slightly when the 2,000-pound fish shot into the sea.

"One away!" the shout came from the forward tubes through the open companionways.

Carlo could see the wake of his fish slanting through the water, leaving a telltale line of bubbles.

Carlo pulled away and motioned Lutfi to the periscope. For a moment Lutfi saw nothing, then the wave subsided and he picked out the small tanker three hundred yards from the massive ship. The entire side of the small tanker suddenly erupted. Large chunks of metal and plates shot into the sky.

A billowing, flaming secondary explosion shook the ship.

Smoke and flames covered the craft from bow to stern. She rolled toward the hidden killer, broke in two and sank under the smoke-choked waves.

A burning oil slick two hundred yards square raged where the ship had been.

"Direct hit. Good shooting," Lutfi said, coming away from the glass. "She broke in two and sank within sixty seconds," he announced.

A cheer went up from the men in the U-boat. Lutfi went to the radio shack, a small open area directly across from the commander's open quarters.

"You've been monitoring the *Contessa*'s radio transmissions," he said to the dark clean-shaven youth.

"Yes, sir. We have their frequency. We're ready to transmit at any time."

"Bring her up, Carlo. I want Captain Running to see us. Keep your bow aimed straight at the middle of the *Contessa*."

Lutfi picked up the microphone and pushed the talk button.

"This is *Hunter* calling the *Contessa*. Calling the *Contessa*. Can you hear me? Over." Lutfi spoke in English now, with a faint British accent to the words.

Lutfi let up on the Talk button and listened. He was ready to repeat the call when an excited voice answered.

"Yes, this is the *Contessa*. Who is calling?"

"This is the *Hunter*, the submarine that's surfacing 500 meters off your port side." He felt the U-boat break the surface. "Check to port and look at us before you reply."

There were ninety seconds of dead air, then the receiver came to life, a voice crackling with anger.

"Yes, I see you. This is the *Contessa*'s captain speaking. Are you the murderers who just killed fifteen fine men? Did you sink the *Crude Lady*? You'll all hang for this. I'll see to that personally."

Lutfi pushed the talk button and chuckled. "Captain Running, you must learn to control your emotions. It is a sign of weakness. You're lucky—it could have been the *Contessa* we fired at instead of the small tanker. You could be the one swimming in a sea of burning crude. I have instructions, I have *orders* for you.

"Captain Running, you and your ship, the *Contessa*, are now under my control. If you do not do as I tell you, your ship will be torpedoed. My gunners have their fingers on the fire buttons of four torpedoes at this very moment. Any attempt to attack my vessel will result in the immediate firing of those four lethal weapons. Is that clear, Captain?"

"You would never do it. You wouldn't spill all this oil. . . ."

"Just the way I wouldn't sink that small tanker? I can and I will blow you out of the water, Captain Running. I win either way. Now, are you ready to listen to reason?"

"What is your price?"

"Your ship, Captain Running."

"No."

"You give her up to my prize crew, or we sink her here and now."

"We have a torpedo deflection net. You can't hurt us."

"Bravado, Captain. It's the same net that protected the *Crude Lady* and it will protect you about as well. Lower your captain's gig into the water at once and send her to pick up me and my crew at this submarine. You will lower your boarding ladder and float and prepare to receive my crew. Or we will sink you and spread a million and a half tons of crude along the shores of all countries around the Mediterranean. The choice, the *responsibility*, for the decision, is yours, Captain Running."

"There are destroyers racing toward your position at this second," Running said in desperation. "I can't stop them."

"If you don't stop them, Captain Running," Lutfi said, "I'll fire my torpedoes in exactly thirty seconds. In case they're not monitoring this transmission, you had better warn them away at once. You now have twenty-five seconds."

Lutfi yelled toward the bridge where he had sent Carlo.

"Carlo, do you see any destroyers nearby?"

"Yes, sir. One, but she's slowing, turning now, sharply. She's stopping, well off."

Lutfi smiled. It had worked. Planning. Planning, experts, and guts of steel, that's all it took. The captain would give up his ship. He had no other choice. The destroyers would keep their distance, they had no other choice.

Lutfi had planned it that way.

6

The telephone rang only once in Mack Bolan's room in the French officers' barracks near Marseille before he answered it. At once he was fully awake, and knew who was speaking after the first two words.

"Colonel Phoenix, you were right. Lutfi has just taken command of the *Contessa*."

The nightfighter began pulling on clothes as he listened to a brief version of how Lutfi captured the largest tanker in the world.

"He's on board her now, Perkins?"

"Yes. First he threatened to torpedo the tanker. Then once aboard he claims he put a thousand pounds of C-4 plastique at various spots around the *Contessa*. If anyone attempts to attack him or try to retake the *Contessa*, he will detonate the bombs and blow the tanker apart. He says he will trigger all the C-4 bombs at once with a radio controlled detonator. The slightest pressure on a red button will do the job."

Bolan grunted. "So what the hell are we doing about this? Where's the field general headquarters on this mission? Where are you?"

"I'm at our Paris embassy. The headquarters down there are on the U.S. destroyer *Streib*, which is standing a half mile off the *Contessa*. I've had orders from my director that you are to handle this affair for the United States, *carte blanche*."

"I'm moving."

"I've arranged for an assault helicopter for you there at Marseille. No U.S. choppers are available and this one is the best the French have. They call it the *Sauterelle*, the Grasshopper."

"Roger, Perkins. I'll want some equipment from you. I'll radio the list to you once we're airborne. These items I want within a few hours. No substitutes, no excuses. Probably get them right here in Marseille. Chopper them out to the *Streib*. Out."

Bolan had dressed in a one-piece black skinsuit. He pounded on Grimaldi's door and found the pilot already dressed. Jack took one look at the blacksuit and grabbed his hat.

"Must be cooking," Grimaldi said. Bolan filled him in as they ran outside and caught a jeep to the flight line.

Five minutes later they were in the air. The French chopper had good firepower: rocket pods, all loaded, twin-mounted machine guns, grenade launchers and a front-firing 40mm cannon. The bird was big enough to hold twelve fully armed troopers. A French pilot lifted her off, but after two minutes in the air, Grimaldi had been checked out and was flying the bird.

Bolan had worked out his supply list and radioed it to the American Embassy by a land-line linkup through the French base. He gave Perkins the list and signed off.

Ahead they saw the small flotilla, the huge tanker, two destroyers circling her, two other destroyers hovering a half mile away, and a smudge on the emerald green Mediterranean sea that was long, black and low in the water.

Grimaldi set down the chopper on the landing pad of a U.S. destroyer, and the warrior hurried to meet a U.S. Navy full lieutenant and two French officers. All three saluted.

"Colonel Phoenix, sir. Lieutenant Cleater. We understand you're in charge of this operation. If you wish, I can brief you on developments within the past two hours." He introduced the two Frenchmen.

"Thanks, Cleater. Let's keep it informal. Have the hijackers made any demands yet?"

"Yes, sir. This way, please. We have it on tape."

They went to the bridge where a seaman punched up a tape recording of the hijacker's demands.

"Attention, France, England, and America. This is the new captain of the *Contessa*. I have complete control of the ship. I have a submarine ready to torpedo this oil factory at a moment's notice and, also, I have strategically placed a thousand pounds of plastic explosive in vital areas of the tanker. I can blast the ship apart and spew a million and a half tons of crude oil all over your coastlines.

"This is what I demand. One: you will make no attempts to recover this vessel. Two: within eighteen hours you will deliver 200 million U.S. dollars worth of pure gold. Three: you will release the forty-two political prisoners I have listed in a dispatch now available at the U.S. Embassy in Paris. Four: you will make no attempt to interfere with my team's departure, or to board the *Contessa* for twelve hours after we leave. If you board the vessel before that time, she will be blown into a dozen pieces. I will expect your response within two hours.''

The tape ended and the Executioner scowled. "He doesn't want much." There was a pause. "The submarine, is it a World War II German U-boat?''

Lieutenant Cleater nodded. "From what we can see it's one of the later models made near the end of the war, with a few alterations. We've had a high-resolve zoom lens on it since we arrived. It looks like a museum piece straight out of 1945.''

"No special radar or underwater detection gear?''

"None we can see sir.''

One of the French officers shook his head. "My government requires the strictest of compliance with the terrorist's demands so the oil is not released.''

"Tell him anything you want to," Bolan said. "The diplomacy end of it is your job. The man on the *Contessa* is called Lutfi. He's a gambler. His threats to torpedo the *Contessa* are a bluff. He won't blow up the tanker as long as he is still on board. Now, we'll take out the sub first.''

"We can furnish you with a ten-man underwater demolition team," Lieutenant Cleater said.

Bolan shook his head. "No thanks. A ten-man team would be too easy to spot. I'll go in alone. Cleater, do you have an underwater electric sled?''

Cleater nodded an affirmative.

"Bring it on deck. Has that chop developed yet? It was supposed to kick up a little by noon.''

"Light chop, sir. A few whitecaps showing."

"Good. Get me a wet suit, a water-tight carrying bag for arms and grenades, some side arms and extra magazines for my Beretta. I'll also need two cubes of C-4 plastique. Let's move. I'd say Lutfi has a few surprises planned for us long before his eighteen hour deadline is up."

"What do we do about his demands, sir?" Lieutenant Cleater asked.

"Follow through. Pass it along to the diplomats and tell the bankers to start getting the gold together. Get the negotiations on the prisoners under way, and get some commercial-radio newscasts planted with stories. Handle it however you want to, but don't give him the gold. We are in French waters. I'll leave the diplomacy up to the three of you."

Twelve minutes later Mack Bolan slid into the cool waters of the Mediterranean. He sank beneath the light chop and tested his scuba gear. Then he touched the underwater sled's On button and felt the sled surge forward, silently towing him along at three knots. The sled was an ES-Mark 4, an experimental model the Navy was using on field testing. It was nothing but a large tube with handles on the side. The tube was eight inches in diameter and three feet long, packed with high-energy electric batteries and an eight-inch multibladed propeller that churned the water silently but produced almost no bubbles. It was painted a sleek gray and was hard to spot in the sea.

The American combatman had not consciously outlined an attack plan. He knew what had to be done, so he would do it. In a small soft-plastic bag tied to a loop in his black wetsuit he carried the two quarter pounds of C-4 plastique. He would use them first.

On the half-mile trip Bolan saw a few big fish in the clear waters, but no sharks. He passed through a school of six-inch-long darters that looked like sea perch; there were thousands of them.

He surfaced once, barely letting his face break into the air, to check his direction. The sub was a few degrees to his left, now no more than three hundred yards away. He saw a sentry pacing the forward deck. Bolan ducked underwater and turned on the sled again.

The sleek black hull of the steel-plated sub materialized in front of him. He had forgotten how small these old boats were.

He turned off the sled and felt no current. Good. Bolan again switched on the sled and powered along side the U-boat to the large rudder and the shiny brass propellers at the stern. Both were still as the craft rolled slightly on the surface.

Bolan quickly took half of one of the blocks of C-4 and mashed it against the shaft just behind the propeller, then did the same to the other one.

He inserted a waterproof pencil timer-detonator in each one, set them both for two minutes and pushed the start slides.

Bolan powered the sled, and moved away from the stern toward the bow of the U-boat, away from the upcoming blast. With both propellers blown off the shafts, the pigboat would be dead in the water, unable to maneuver into firing position. All she would be able to do then was float with the tide or sink.

The numbers were coming down fast now. Bolan edged toward the surface. He hit the side of the U-boat and pulled his head out of the water five seconds before the blast. He did not want to lose his eardrums from the underwater concussion.

The explosion rippled at him through the hull, which he held for support. The force rocketed through the water and he felt it all over his body.

When the last shock waves had passed, he submerged the sled to just below the surface, waiting for a reaction on board.

Bolan unhooked the waterproof sack from the sled, tied the craft to the hydroplanes, and got out of the scuba gear and tanks, which he tied to the sled. He saw no one on board. Where was the sentry?

He pushed the bag of tools up the sloping side of the sub's bow and scrambled after it. When he reached the heavy antenna line, he pulled himself higher on the wet plates, clearing Big Thunder, the silver .44 Auto-Mag, from its waterproof bag as he did so.

The sentry came running from the stern, evidently returning from investigating the explosion. He was wide-eyed, carried his rifle carelessly, and moved toward the open forward hatch. They saw each other at the same time. Bolan lifted the minicannon and fired before the terrorist could shoulder his rifle. The heavy lead slug caught the guy in the chest. The slug pushed two ribs through the guy's heart as it turned sideways, ripping lungs apart before exiting out the back.

The body jolted sideways, sprawling facedown. The automatic rifle hit the deck, skittered to one side and slid into the green blue waters.

Bolan's attention turned to the torpedo loading hatch. It was open. He saw a head appear, then duck out of sight. Before Bolan could react, a man leaned out of the hatch with an automatic rifle in his hands and blazed away in unaimed frenzy.

Bolan's .44 spoke twice, slamming twin death messengers at the terrorist, pulverizing his right eye, pulping brain tissue and gray matter.

A figure on the bridge chattered off six shots from an automatic, but all the lead missed the nightfighter who had rolled once and come up in a two-fisted position to hammer two lead widowmakers into the gunman's neck, snapping his spine.

A hand reached from below to close the hatch cover. Bolan jerked up the Beretta 93-R machine pistol and coughed three silent rounds into the hand, splattering fingers against the unyielding metal. A scream billowed through the Mediterranean morning.

Before the wet-suited black figure could move down the submarine deck, a round object soared from the hatch and bounced toward him. With a combat veteran's instinctive reaction, Bolan swiped at the incoming grenade as he would a handball, slapping it into the water where it exploded harmlessly. Even before the sound echoed away, the Executioner was on his feet, charging the hatch, with two grenades ready, pins pulled.

He dropped both grenades down the U-boat torpedo-loading hatch.

The twin explosions came as one, spewing hot shrapnel and smoke from the opening.

Then all was quiet.

Bolan checked the bow of the ship killer. It had swung in the current and no longer aimed its death fish at the huge tanker.

Bolan edged up to the side of the torpedo loading hatch, thrust his head over the void to steal a look below and pulled back sharply. He saw only the mangled, shredded remains of a man.

The nightfighter took time to loop the Beretta's lanyard around his neck and to grab two more grenades. Was the sub dead? Could he leave it? He had to get to the supertanker.

But the Executioner knew the U-boat still had those stingers in its forward tubes. She could still swing back in the current and aim herself at the *Contessa* again. He still had to deliver the coup de grace.

A scraping noise came from the bridge and a shadow appeared, then vanished. Bolan threw a grenade. The small bomb hit inside the tub-like bridge and exploded, bringing a cry of pain that quickly faded into silence. The combatman dropped one more handbomb down the hatch, and as soon as the explosion echoed past him, he hurried down the hole, pulling his bag of arms with him.

The Beretta 93-R preceded him, and he flashed a burst into the room below him even though he saw no target. His rounds brought answering fire from the open passageway that ran through the center of the boat. Bolan sent another half-dozen rounds searching for the gunman. He knew he'd found his target from the deathly scream.

Now he crouched behind a metal bulkhead. He was in the bow compartment where torpedoes were stored over and under eight bunks. In this area the deadly fish were loaded into the tubes and fired. All four torpedo tube doors were closed, probably blown clear of water and ready for a surface-fire command.

Behind him was a water-tight compartment door that was partly open. He pushed the heavy metal door, and as it swung inward he jumped to one side.

A dozen melting lead rounds poured through the opening.

He could see the craft's head to one side and a narrow passage into some quarters with bunks and lockers. The Executioner fired a dozen rounds through the open door and heard a wail.

He was back to house-to-house fighting—clearing every hiding spot as he went. Bolan took another frag grenade from his bag, pulled the pin and threw the bomb through the door. The explosion in the confined space deafened the warrior, but when the hot shrapnel quit zinging, he rushed into the crew quarters and on through to the wardroom and officer's mess.

There was no one alive in either area. Two dead youths, barely out of their teens, were sprawled in a deadly stretching exercise on the floor and over one bunk. Both still clutched handguns.

The bulkhead behind the officer's mess was solid and barred by a metal door. The heavy steel pressure door was hinged to swing away from Bolan.

He slapped a half square of C-4 plastique on the latch side and pushed in a timer-detonator set at thirty seconds.

Bolan started the timer and rushed back into the torpedo room.

Just as he arrived, a man crawled from one of the torpedo tubes. Bolan shot him in the head with the silenced Beretta. A second torpedo-tube cover moved outward.

Bolan rammed it shut and locked it in place, and when he saw a green light glow over the tube, he hit the firing button.

He felt the compressed air slam forward, propelling the terrorist hiding in the tube toward the exterior doors, mashing him into jelly, crushing every bone in his body, then spewing him into the Mediterranean.

Before the hissing of the firing stopped, the whole U-boat shuddered with the massive, ear-killing explosion of the locked water-tight door.

The Executioner shook his head twice after the blast—the concussion had rattled through him like an earthquake through a tree. For a moment he saw double; he closed his eyes tightly. His head cleared and he lifted the machine pistol and ran forward. The door into the commander's quarters and the radio shack hung by a single hinge.

In the radio shack a man with a crewcut held his hands over his ears. His eyes bulged in fear as he saw Bolan. He scratched for the side arm on his right hip. The Beretta coughed three deadly times and eternity swallowed the radioman.

There were no corridors or rooms here as on surface ships, just an open passage down the middle of the boat with living quarters and facilities overlapping. Bolan heard sound coming from the next open hatch.

He knew he should be near the control room under the bridge and conning tower. The sound turned into screaming in Italian. An automatic weapon fired through the door. Bolan ducked behind the bulkhead near the radio shack. When the firing stopped, he leaned around and pushed the Beretta through the opening and emptied a 20-round magazine into the area. He heard glass break, a moan and a long sigh, then a death rattle.

The nightfighter waited for two minutes before he moved. There was no other sound. Slowly he edged around the door. Two men lay on the floor, shirtless and bathed in blood. Each held a grenade, but the pins were still firmly in place.

Bolan charged through the rest of the compartments: the control room, the petty-officer quarters, the galley, the engine room and the electric-motor room. He ran all the way to the torpedo room in the stern and found no one else alive. He walked back to the bow and the forward torpedo room.

A soft scraping overhead at the bow alerted him. Someone was on deck. He climbed through the hatch and saw a man near the bow, working in the water.

The sea sled!

Six rounds from the Beretta cut short the terrorist's escape attempt. His bullet-riddled body floated for a moment, arms swinging with the gentle current, then the face disappeared under the water and a moment later vanished as the mortal remains sank into the sea, there to join the marine food chain.

Bolan looked at the sub, the tool a terrorist had used to capture the big tanker. For just a moment he wanted to open the sea cocks and let the old warrior go to the bottom where she could rest in peace and not be hijacked for any other such mission. He tied his tools in the waterproof bag and slid into the water near the sled. It was not damaged. He put on his tanks and his mask. He would leave the fate of the U-boat to the French navy.

Bolan pushed off from the sub, started the sea sled and motored on the surface to the nearest American destroyer in fifteen minutes.

As he was climbing the ladder to the destroyer *Streib*, Bolan found a U.S. Navy commander giving a fifteen-man UDT its final instructions.

The Executioner took off his scuba and listened for a minute. Then, using his parade-grounds bellow, he stopped the commander.

"Commander, those men are not going anywhere. You and I need to have a short talk. Now."

The commander jumped, turned. Surprise, followed by anger, flooded his face. He marched to where Bolan stood, his face growing redder by the second.

Ready to explode, he stopped inches from the Executioner. His voice was low but deadly.

"Look, asshole. I don't know who the hell you are, but you don't give *me* orders on a U.S. Navy ship. Is that damn clear? I'm the ranking naval officer on this mission."

Bolan laughed softly. "Commander, you were never in command of this ship or this mission. You only thought you were. My name is Colonel John Phoenix, and I am in command here. You have any trouble with that, you talk to Lieutenant Cleater; he is second-in-command when I'm off site. You are excused, Commander, I don't want to see you on deck again." Bolan turned to the frogmen, some of whom wore wide grins.

"Party's over men, no mission. Think of it as a dry run. That maniac over there on the *Contessa* would blow her up for sure if he saw all of us coming. We're not going to give him an excuse. Not yet. Get unsuited and relax. Lieutenant Cleater is in command here when I'm not on board."

The lieutenant materialized from a passageway, and his young face was serious as he dismissed the men. When he approached Bolan, there was more than a touch of worry in his eyes.

"Sorry, Colonel. He's my senior and came over from the other destroyer. There wasn't anything I could do."

"Forget it. He should be under wraps now. If he isn't, let me know and we'll have him commanding a captain's gig. We've got to move on to phase two now."

The ship's speaker broke in with a transmission.

"This is the new captain of the *Contessa*. I have a message for you. I know you have attacked my submarine. I can't reach my men there by radio. If any of my people are harmed, I will kill one of the crewmen from the *Contessa* for each of my men hurt.

Are you total fools? You say you are cooperating, getting the gold, working on the prisoner freedom— then you attack me!'' The voice had risen to a high pitch at the end of the sentence. When the voice continued, there was an even, steady tone that sent a terrible chill through Bolan.

"Remember, if any of my men are killed, I will retaliate by executing the same number of crewmen from this vessel. Your deadline is approaching. Meet my demands, or suffer the ultimate in consequences.''

Lieutenant Cleater swore.

"Forget it, Cleater,'' Bolan said. "There was no way to keep him from finding out he'd lost the U-boat. I've been expecting some kind of retaliation on the hostages. Did you get my packages from Paris?''

The young officer nodded. "Are you really going to try to use it?''

"Yes. It has to work, otherwise you, I and the commander over there will be spending our next five-year hitch cleaning crude oil off the French coastline. Bring everything to the fantail and let's get started.''

Bolan had figured that this was the only way to get on board the *Contessa* undetected. She rose seventy-three feet from waterline to scuppers. It would be a tough go for a mountain climber, or even a top-notch UDT with magnetic climbing handles. No, this way had to work. It was up to Bolan to get onto the tanker and put Lutfi away, without letting him push that little red radio-detonator button.

Bolan nodded to himself. Here he was sitting on millions of dollars worth of guided missiles and rockets and electronic gear, with dozens of top-quality Navy fighter planes not far away with air-to-ground missiles, yet it all came down to one man who had to go in and do the job.

One man. There was no chance that the military could do it without Lutfi blowing apart the tanker.

It was a one-man job.

And he was the man.

7

The next few hours were frantic for Mack Bolan.

He had returned from the submarine just past one in the afternoon and eaten a fast meal.

Lutfi's diatribes continued on the radio, denouncing everyone on earth.

Then he brought out a *Contessa* crewman and shot him ten times in the chest.

There was no chance he had faked the execution. The destroyer's long-zoom-lens video camera brought the death throes of the seaman to full screen for the video recorder.

Some of the men in the common room thought the execution was fake. Bolan knew better. He had seen too many men die. He went back to the fantail and continued to work on his new weapons.

A fresh demand came through on the radio from Lutfi.

"To the murderers who killed my men. You will pay. First you must pay double in gold—I now demand 400 million. Those of us who work for the freedom of the world's downtrodden people will never forget this criminal act against these heroic freedom fighters. We demand our pound of flesh. One crewman from the *Contessa* will be executed each hour until darkness. I know you are watching with powerful cameras. Show the world that Lutfi never sleeps, that Lutfi will soon be an international force to contend with, to respect. Yes, to *respect*."

The nightfighter scowled. One execution an hour. It was nearly four in the afternoon. One, perhaps, two more before dusk.

The Executioner concentrated on the device in front of him. The large package had arrived an hour before he returned from the submarine. He had found willing, experienced volunteers to help him— two sun-splashed youths from California. Soon the full-sized parasail was laid out on deck.

"You've flown one before?" the blond-thatched young sailor asked. Bolan nodded quickly. "Remember, on takeoff be sure to keep the tow rope as tight as you can, and be sure the boat doesn't go too fast, otherwise you're in big trouble. We've used a tow lots of times from a pickup. We had to watch speed most of all. And we never used to tow over ten miles per hour." The youth paused and made sure the harness was attached correctly to the lead lines. "The way I see it, sir, you have only one shot at it. If you don't get enough altitude, or if you spin out and splash down, it'll be hell just finding you out there in that chop."

Those had been the Executioner's thoughts exactly, but there was no other practical way to board the *Contessa* silently and unobserved. Lutfi was already enraged. One more incident might push him into the most murderous irrationality. Then the creep would forget all his plans and blow up the tanker just for the hell of it.

A few minutes later the parasail was ready for testing.

They let the parachute fill with air, and Bolan hung ten feet off the deck on a tether, flying into the freshening wind. Then he sank gently back to the fantail.

Bolan worked out the method of launch, and he talked with the coxswain of the special powerboat that would pull him.

Jack Grimaldi stood in the background shaking his head. "That thing looks too damn risky, Colonel. I can put you down on the far end of the *Contessa* all safe and sound. We know I can get you in there and get you out, so why gamble?"

"We can't go in hard, Jack. It's got to be a soft probe for as long as possible. When it goes hard, it goes. Until that time, the more I can find out, and the closer I can come to locating and neutralizing Lutfi and his electronic detonator, the better. I'll make it, Jack. I want you warmed up and ready to come in for support. I'm going to need it. Can you give me a five-minute response time?"

"Right, no sweat. I still...." The pilot lifted his arms in resignation and turned away, knowing he could not change Mack's mind.

Before dark they had rehearsed the takeoff three times. Coxswain Tom Mallory piloted the special speedboat, idling it alongside the fantail, then playing out the five hundred feet of tough eighth-inch nylon line until it came tight around the ship's cleat. The twelve-foot aluminum boat was powered by a silent forty-five horsepower electric outboard motor.

Bolan had ordered the motor and batteries with the parasail from Paris. It would move the boat silently and quickly and get Bolan high enough to land on the far end of the *Contessa*—he hoped.

By the time the last dry run was over it was dark. From the bridge came the word: the *Contessa* was lighted like a sidewalk carnival on payday. Bolan would have no trouble finding his landing pad.

"Let's do it," the Executioner said. The 93-R hung from the lanyard around his neck. Big Thunder was tied down on his right hip. He wore his blacksuit, combat webbing and a combat pack filled with weapons. On his left hip rode a K-Bar fighting knife. He was going in soft and would maintain it soft as long as possible.

The blond kid from California buckled the night-fighter into the harness.

"Hey, man. Wish I was going with you. Remember, there are no updrafts out there, so whatever altitude you get on the tow is it. You sink or you fly depending on how fast that gig pulls you. Got your flash?"

Bolan nodded.

"One flash toward the gig and he speeds up a knot, which pulls me higher and faster," Bolan said, going over the game plan one final time. "Two flashes and he'll cut back a knot."

Bolan checked his equipment once more, saw that the nylon tow line was securely fastened to the shroud lines and that the line was tight and slack by turns around the cleat.

The boy from California unwrapped the line from

the cleat when it was slack, and let it play out slowly over the top of the rail.

Bolan watched the line tighten. Then he blinked the flash one time toward the electrically powered boat.

The sailor watched the line become tight and waved at Bolan. The nightfighter was thirty feet back from the drop-off of the destroyer's fantail. He would walk or run into the wind until he took off.

8

"Go," the kid called.

Bolan felt the rope tighten, urging him forward. He took three steps and sensed a stronger tug on the harness. Two more running steps and he was kicking nothing but air as he soared over the stern at an angle sharper than he had expected.

Before he looked down, the ship was already behind him. The soft Mediterranean night air swept over his body. The sudden ascent slowed, then he climbed gradually. The gig below made a sweeping turn, heading for the tanker. Bolan flew into the turn, moving his body, tilting the wing. He needed more altitude.

Less than a half mile ahead he saw the glowing lights of the *Contessa* and its broad, flat top. Bolan turned on his flashlight, making a long, continual beam. He switched it off. Slowly he felt the increased pressure on the line and knew he was climbing more. His frame of reference was still confused. He could not see the launch below, but he realized he was closer to it, therefore higher. The *Contessa*'s deck was his focal point now. He knew it was seventy-three feet off the water. He had to maintain that much altitude, and one chance was all he had.

The nightfighter estimated the distance again. By this time he was halfway there, less than a quarter mile from the glaring island of steel. More altitude. He pushed the light on again for one long flash. The surge was greater this time, and ahead he saw a searchlight on the tanker begin a computer-programmed search pattern.

The lift carried him higher and higher, and far below he knew the power boat moved with its silent electric motor, but he could neither see it nor hear it.

More than halfway there. They had designed no clever approach; they would drive straight at the tanker and, when almost there, make a sweeping turn. Bolan would use the control lines on one side to dump some of the air and drift in the desired direction. In that manner he could swing well to the side of the powerboat and land on the deck while the boat slipped past the stationary bow.

The searchlight pattern ceased.

The *Contessa* leaped at him, less than three hundred yards away, he guessed. The boat below began to make the sweeping turn.

He needed to move left. He grabbed the shroud line on the left and tugged it gently. Nothing happened. He pulled it harder, and his stomach jolted as the left side of the chute spilled air. He slipped to that side until the chute filled again.

The *Contessa* was looming now. She was huge, much bigger looking when night lighted.

Bolan was at least fifty feet over the top of the deck. He would signal to slow down the moment he was over the edge of the tanker.

He was close. The Executioner stared at the gigantic ship. Most supertankers have a huge expanse of flat deck, only half covered with miles of loading/unloading pipes to pump petroleum to the holds. The *Contessa* was one large maze of pipes.

The specs he had read mentioned the masses of pipes, but they had been minimized. As he stared ahead through the soft mist, it looked as though the huge deck was almost entirely covered with a metal network. Down through the center of the ship lay a metal walkway that topped the distribution system, and directly under the walkway ran a foot-thick pipe filled with fire-fighting foam.

Because of the size of the vessel, the holds had been built with a certain amount of give in them, and each had a separate hold cover. This resulted in gullies and ravines between the holds. They were four feet deep and about that wide, all well below the maze of pipes, ladders and walkways, and there were even a dozen crossover bridges that extended from side to side over all the piping.

As Bolan sailed toward the tangle, he realized he had found a perfect sniper's lair. He could hide among those pipes and gullies for as long as he wanted.

The darkened distance almost fooled him. He was still too high. Bolan flashed twice at the boat with his light and felt the slowdown. He dropped gently toward the deck. By that time he was over the deck and he flashed a continuous beam. The boat stopped. He sank down softly and touched an open space on deck. Bolan at once unhooked the quick release on the harness and slid out of it. He was down. The dark parasail, relieved of its burden, sprang back into the air and a moment later vanished into the sky.

Bolan stood on a little island of decking, with large pipes on both sides and one of the gullies a dozen feet away. He ran lightly over the rough surface of the steel tank top and dropped silently into the four-foot deep valley.

Bolan crouched and listened. Had anyone heard or seen him? He held his breath and heard the sound of footsteps...coming closer. Then a voice called softly in Italian. Bolan loosened the silenced Beretta and held it ready. With his left hand he drew the K-Bar fighting knife.

He had reached over his right shoulder with his left hand and unsnapped a fastener on the K-Bar's scabbard and let the big blade ease out of the upside-down leather. The inch-and-a-half-thick blade was five inches long and made of high-quality stainless steel tempered to a fine cutting edge with an inch Bowie double-cutting edge on the tip.

The Executioner crouched in the depression between hold covers, and when the sentry came closer, the hellgrounder could see him plainly. Bolan waited. The guard walked toward him.

The Executioner waited until the terrorist was almost upon him, then leaped up and thrust the big knife chest high. The sentry saw him at the last second and tried to lift his rifle; but by then the K-Bar had razored through a light shirt, grated off a rib and pierced tissue as it plunged through the lower half of the terrorist's heart, dispatching him with only a small gurgle of bloody froth. Bolan caught the body as it fell. He draped it over his shoulder and carried the dead terrorist toward the railing. Bolan heaved the body over the side.

The hellgrounder pulled three frag grenades from his pack and clipped them to his combat webbing. With the Beretta firmly in hand, he headed toward a large splash of light up the long deck.

Bolan moved at a combat-assault pace, watching carefully on both sides, keeping the Beretta ready. His rubber-soled boots made no noise on the deck.

Twice he detoured to avoid puddles of light on the acres of the deck, piping and hold gullies.

Near the third floodlight he saw the glow of a cigarette. Silently he worked around the yellow light and came up behind the sentry. There was no way he could get any closer without being seen. Bolan lifted the Beretta and it coughed out one kiss of doom. The slug slashed through bone, tissue and cells just over the sentry's left ear, and he toppled off his perch, dead before he hit the steel deck.

The nightfighter had worked his way almost to the superstructure when a siren sounded. Then a voice from a nearby speaker sputtered in Italian. The Executioner's Italian was not perfect, but he caught the drift of the announcement. One of the sentries had not checked in on schedule, a three-man enforcement squad would investigate at once. Bolan's ice-blue eyes squinted. So far his attack was still soft.

So far.

9

The Executioner moved like a shadow down the long deck, filtering through the random patches of darkness.

He saw two, three-man search parties, but froze in deep shadows under the pipes as the men hurried by. All carried guns; some carried the worried, unsure expressions of newcomers to violent death. It was here that all the rhetoric, bravado and billowing emotions of a terrorist cause coalesced into the sudden violent action that makes death a constant, leering companion.

The big guy avoided the terrorists as he moved toward the towering mass of the superstructure perched at the far end of the long vessel. Across the final stretch, his approach had to change. He would be in the open, and he would either have to bluff his way across or kill whoever challenged him.

Bolan's primary mission remained the same—to find Lutfi and relieve him of the electronic detonator, and to do it without setting off the bombs he was sure the terrorist had planted. But as Bolan closed in on his target he knew the madman might also turn on the pumps and dump crude into the Mediterranean. There was no reason to doubt that

Lutfi would do this—if he thought it would help his cause. Preventing such a spill was Bolan's second mission once the electronic detonator was captured or destroyed. Beyond that, he played his priorities by ear.

Bolan jumped back into the deep shadows as two men hurried by and raced through a door that led into the first level of the superstructure. It had been built at the stern of the ship, with a narrow open deck on each side. Stairs or elevators evidently led to the upper floors. When the two men were long past, Bolan lifted the Beretta machine pistol, walked across the open twenty yards to the door and stepped inside.

He found stairs stretching upward.

The Executioner went up the steps two at a time, opened a door marked #2 and eased into a hallway. The hallway ran the width of the superstructure, with several doors leading off it. Bolan knew from his diagram study that the bridge was on the top—the seventh—floor, along with the communications rooms and the officers' quarters.

Ten feet ahead a door opened. The man who came out called to someone in the room, looking back at the person he was speaking to. When the man turned, Bolan pressed the Beretta's muzzle against his heart.

"Aiutate," the man screamed. The Beretta jumped twice as the two 9mm slugs tore through bone and heart. Bolan caught the dead man as he fell and pushed him back into the room and onto a carpeted floor. The terrorist's cry for help had alerted two men in the small room. One bare-chested

young man reached for a .45 automatic on his bunk. The other man, larger and older, simply lifted both hands skyward out of respect for the machine pistol.

Bolan ice-eyed the first man off the .45, then motioned for both to sit on the floor in the middle of the room. *"Sedete,"* he said. Bolan tied up the young man, then pulled the older one to a standing position.

"Capisci?" Bolan asked, nudging the man toward the door. There was no response. "Lutfi?" the night-fighter asked, and the older terrorist nodded. Bolan frisked him quickly, found a short-barreled .38 fully loaded. He pushed it into his combat pack. The hallway was empty. They went out the door; Bolan stayed directly behind the terrorist who knew where he was going. They walked to the stairwell that Bolan had just left and climbed. The terrorist's head was down; he would not meet Bolan's stare. They went up the stairs to the fourth floor. On the landing of the fifth floor, the Italian exploded to life, slamming Bolan halfway over the railing—with nothing but a five-story drop below him.

The big Italian had the advantage of surprise and position, but the Executioner knew more hand-to-hand fighting tricks. Bolan grabbed an arm, bent it backward, spun the Italian around and forced him half over the rail. At the same time he looped the Beretta's lanyard around the terrorist's soft neck and pulled. The terrorist choked off a scream, then struggled, kicking, flailing his arms, gasping for breath. Bolan jammed his knee into the man's back and increased the pressure on the tough nylon cord.

Gradually the thrashing arms and legs weakened and slowed. At last they sagged and went limp.

The Executioner tilted the body over the railing, unlooped the Beretta cord and let the corpse fall.

A scream billowed from below as the corpse splattered on the deck. Sirens seemed to go off over the whole ship. Quickly Bolan stripped a grenade off his webbing, pulled the pin and dropped the bomb down the center of the stairwell. It would create a distraction, help hold any pursuers in the stairs. Bolan trusted the ship's builders were balanced thinkers and had put stairways on both sides. . . .

He opened the door to the fifth floor and sprinted across the corridor toward the far side. There were rooms on both sides. As stealthily as possible the Executioner moved downward. He needed to relocate and do some planning, now that the probe had turned hard. Would Lutfi blow up the *Contessa*? Bolan's reasoning remained: the terrorist would not push the button until he got exactly what he wanted.

The Executioner made it to the second floor before he heard anyone on the stairs. The footsteps were above him. He continued down the steps and opened the door on the deck level.

No one was outside. Where were they? Moving the prisoners? They knew he was on board, but they were not swarming after him.

Bolan darted to a series of low maintenance sheds near the superstructure and hid in the shadows. For a moment he picked up some intel. The search seemed concentrated on the second floor. He saw two armed men run forward. Bolan moved that way as quietly as he could. He was only fifty feet from the superstructure when he noticed a change in the deck pattern. It was flat and had no pipes. Near the far side, almost attached to the seven-floor area, he saw a two-story building, twenty by thirty feet. The front had a rolling door and as he watched, it lifted.

Two men stood in the area staring into the darkness. Both wore heavy lead-lined suits—radiation-proof gear, including helmets, boots and gloves.

Bolan remembered one line about the *Contessa* from the material he had read on her. She was atomic powered, with her own reactor and her own nuclear plant that could supply enough energy to run a dozen ships this size.

Bolan groaned in frustration. He had not concerned himself before with the propulsion system, because he had no tactical interest in it. Now he knew better. Lutfi was *not* trying to get 400 million dollars worth of gold. He was *not* trying to free political prisoners. Both of those demands were nothing more than clever smoke screens, ploys to buy the time he needed.

What Lutfi really wanted were the nuclear fuel rods used to power the atomic plant deep in the bowels of the ship. The rods contained enriched uranium, enough 238 that could be used as the most vital ingredient of a crude but effective atomic bomb. Lutfi was out to capture sufficient enriched uranium to build himself a small arsenal of atomic weapons, which he could use or threaten to use. Bolan knew his enemy—knew all his enemies—because of his own dire experience as America's leading independent

counterterrorist. Therefore he could anticipate his
enemies in a way that was unique amongst his coun-
trymen. He could smell his enemies' intentions. And
Lutfi, by controlling the awesome power that he
sought, could take over one Third World country
after another, building his power base as he plowed
through Africa and the Middle East. The prospect
stank. With ten atomic bombs, and the knowledge
that he would use them, there would be no way to
stop Lutfi without trading atomic punches.

Transport?

Like any military tactician, Bolan thought of Lutfi's next move. How did the terrorist plan to move
the atomic fuel rods? The submarine had never been
in the transport picture for the rods. It was too small,
no loading access, too restrictive, too slow, too easy
to find and kill.

The *Contessa* herself? Use her as a floating em-
pire? She was stocked for a year. Her atomic fuel
would last for at least two years. Lutfi could con-
struct his atomic-bomb-plant workshops on board,
use the housing, bring in specialists, cruise into warm
waters. But Bolan was doubtful.

Perhaps another ship would meet them and off-
load the bulky lead coffins that held the fuel rods.
Possibly.

Bolan heard footsteps coming toward him. The
two radiation-protected men had vanished into the
building that looked like a large freight elevator. It
was large enough to take in and discharge the fuel
rods, even when they were encased in their lead coffins.

The footsteps came closer. Bolan risked a glance around the corner of the small building.

Bolan brought up the silenced Beretta and pushed it around the corner. The charging terrorist could not see the machine pistol in the darkness.

"Hey," Bolan called. The guncock looked up in time to take one sizzling 9mm whizzer through his mouth. As it exited, the slug carried away a cross section of the terrorist's skull.

Two more terrorists were moving toward the elevator. Bolan knew they were coming as protective security, not because they knew the nightfighter was there.

Meanwhile Bolan recalled the coldness, the disdain that Lutfi showed when he killed the crewman hours earlier. In the same way he had killed the crewman, Lutfi could drop an atomic bomb and detonate it over a city. It would be his way to serve notice that the only way to stop him would be to beat him in an atomic war.

True, Lutfi would lose such a battle. But he would take 100 million innocent people along with him. Lutfi was gambling that a rational world, and conservative world leaders, would never permit such an atomic war to start. They would appease him and he would kick dirt in their faces.

Lutfi had to be stopped before he could steal any fuel rods from the *Contessa*.

The work was easy to spell out. Now how the hell could the job get done?

10

Bolan watched the pair of terrorists who were still working toward the elevator. They split up before they came to the body of their comrade, angling toward the far corners of the building.

He was in an ideal spot—any action had to come through here if Lutfi hoped to get the fuel rods off the ship. Now there was no contest when it came to picking priorities. A full load of crude oil splattered along a thousand miles of beaches would not balance out against 100 million human lives snuffed out in an atomic war. He must watch the fuel-rod exit zone and deny it to the enemy force. Later there would be time to find Lutfi and get his little red box.

The problem of transporting the lead coffins again entered Bolan's thoughts. The solution came to mind with the speed of a death slug. From the data he had studied, he knew the *Contessa* had three chopper landing pads marked on the deck. They were built solidly enough to accept fully loaded military helicopters. Big choppers could haul in or take out atomic fuel rods as needed. Bolan stared at the semi-illuminated deck of the big ship and saw a landing pad fifty feet from the elevator that led to the atomic-fuel-rod storage area. The *Contessa*'s inclusion of chopper pads might have played right into the hijacker's hands.

One of the guards from the far side of the elevator strolled toward Bolan's hiding spot and called softly.

"Vencensz!"

"*Si,*" Bolan hissed.

The other guard came forward, waving as he passed through the spills of light.

"*Sigaretta?*"

"*Si.*"

The terrorists walked closer. Bolan spat silent fire at them. Two smoking Beretta rounds pulverized foreheads, kicking scum into hell in the blink of an eyelash.

Bolan ran forward, found the third guard and splattered his chest with two rounds from the machine pistol. He checked the front of the elevator. The door was closed. On a panel he saw a series of numbered and lettered buttons for opening the door; the panel was electronically coded to report security infractions. The Executioner pulled two cubes of C-4 from his pack and pushed them against the side of the door. He fused them with a timer-detonator, set it for thirty seconds and activated it.

He dashed around the far end of the elevator building until he was thirty yards from the charge. He ducked.

The blast jolted the whole elevator structure, punched the building forward an inch, then let it settle back.

Now his mission was hard. Rock hard. More sirens went off in the distance. He heard a dozen men running toward the blast site. There was no chance he could get to the front to see what damage he had done, but he knew that a half pound of C-4 should put the whole elevator system out of action.

He faded into the inky pools of unlit deck and hatch covers and moved toward the center of the huge tanker. There was far less activity there.

Searchlights bathed the elevator area. More floodlights snapped on until the whole scene was lit up like daytime. Loudspeakers chattered with a steady stream of commands in Italian.

The Executioner tossed aside a used magazine from the Beretta, slid in another 20-rounder and charged the weapon. As he watched the activity boiling around the elevator, he knew he'd figured correctly about the real prize of this hijacking. He decided to check out the bridge.

It took him nearly twenty minutes to work his way back through the center of the ship's dark areas and pipe maze until he arrived at a spot where he could make a dash across open deck to the stairwell on the starboard side of the superstructure. There should be fewer people up there now.

He took the steps three at a time as he charged to the top floor, meeting no one coming down. Bolan pulled a frag grenade from his webbing, left the pin in and cracked open a seventh-floor door. Through a sliver view, he saw a carpeted lounge area with living-room-type furniture and a curved window that overlooked the front quarter mile of the ship and the sea ahead. A door with a porthole of shaded glass led off the lounge. No one was in sight.

The Executioner left the stairwell and ran across the lounge to the inner door. He looked through the porthole, but the smoked glass was too dark for him to see anything. No use coming all this way to the party if he was not going to dance.

Bolan pushed open the door and slid inside. He was in some type of control room. There were dozens of gauges and readout dials in a maze of electronic equipment. Another door led him onward and he pushed it open. One man stood near a second maze of dials—a large compass, an assortment of wind, weather, depth readouts and a hundred other knobs and instruments that Bolan had never seen before. High-powered binoculars hung from his neck. The man turned, his eyes friendly. He was about fifty.

"Where is Lutfi?" Bolan barked, Big Thunder directed at the man's head.

"Below. So, that explosion was your work." The man said it calmly. "I'm Hans Running, captain of the *Contessa*. Lutfi lets me watch over my ship. I'm no threat to him."

Bolan knew immediately from the man's demeanor that he faced friend, not foe. "Lutfi wants to steal your atomic fuel rods," he said.

"Yes. He told me. He's mad, of course."

"Agreed. Is there any other way to get the fuel rods to the deck except by that elevator?"

"None. But in fact your blast probably did not hurt the lift. It has dozens of backup systems. It was built to rigid specs—it would take a hundred pounds of plastique to shut it down."

"I used enough to flatten a ten-room house."

"Someone's coming!"

Bolan swung around, saw the door burst open. Two armed men rushed in. Big Thunder roared twice. Two rounds of 240-grain smoking lead caught both gunmen in the chest, slamming them back through the doorway.

Captain Running winced at the noise in the confined space. Then he motioned. "That way. Out that door and down the far stairs. You can do nothing up here."

The Executioner gave a curt nod of thanks, then ran through another lounge to the stairs. He heard someone below. He waited for the visitor to appear around the landing two floors below. A moment later a man leaned out and stared upward. Bolan pegged off two 3-round bursts, slamming most of the slugs into the interloper. The Executioner charged down the steps, stopped and grabbed the dead man's AK-47 assault rifle, then stormed past and gained the freedom of the deck.

The elevator—was it still working? He had to know.

He began working through the darkness on deck to where he could see the front of the elevator building. It took him five minutes of pipe hopping and crawling through the gullies between holds to get into position. The elevator door was open. Two radiation-protected men stood on the platform talking to a tall man. Bolan wondered if the man they spoke to was Lutfi. A new sound registered in his mind, gradually becoming a recognizable entity. When he realized what it was, he scanned the dark skies.

A heavy chopper was coming in.

So far he had been right, and that was not good. Bolan wished he had more firepower. A Quad-Fifty caliber machine gun groundplower would be about right. . . .

He checked his backpack and found eight more frag grenades, some white phosphorous grenades and four more quarter-pound blocks of C-4 plastique. It might work, but he had to get close enough.

Bolan wormed his way among the hatch covers, under the masses of pipes and maneuvered through the dark and light splotches of deck. He watched the chopper wheel in, level out and land on the pad closest to the elevator. Bolan moved again. He had to get within twenty yards of the chopper, and the whole landing pad was now day bright.

The big bird's cargo doors opened on the side. Twenty-five yards from the chopper a special search-light mount had been constructed, and soon Bolan crouched beneath it, well concealed in the shadows and the piping.

He plastered half a block of plastique around the back side of a frag grenade, leaving room for the handle to pop free to arm the bomb. The explosive stuck fast to the metal. He made sure it would not drop off, then prepared another one as backup.

The pilot had just cut the idle speed of the turning rotors when Bolan pulled the pin on the grenade, let the handle pop off and threw the souped-up bomb at the chopper.

The 4.4 seconds were not quite burned up when the grenade bounced under the nose section of the heli-copter.

A fraction of a second later the grenade exploded.

It acted as a detonator for the plastique, triggering it simultaneously.

The explosion sent shrapnel drilling into the bird, igniting the forward section.

A moment later a fuel tank exploded in a high-octane fire that engulfed the entire aircraft.

The Executioner lay in the valley between the hold covers, waiting for the firelight to die down so he could make his move. He could hear one man screaming in agony, but the voice faded and then was gone. Bolan put the second C-4-laced grenade back in his pack, reloaded Big Thunder, and put a fresh magazine in the 93-R. The AK-47 had a full magazine.

One chopper killed. Now it did not matter if the elevator worked or not. With no chopper, Lutfi would need an alternate transport plan.

Before Bolan could calm his racing heartbeat, he heard a sound in the distance—choppers, several this time.

He watched in frustration as three more of the Huey-type birds soon swung in. They hesitated, then landed at different chopper pads.

He could see plainly in the landing lights that two of the birds were gunships, bristling with firepower.

Sometimes things went Bolan's way, sometimes they did not. When they did not, it was his job to turn around the odds.

It would just be harder that way.

A *lot* harder.

11

Mack Bolan stared at one of the choppers and for a moment he was back in Nam. Dressed in brown-and-green-camouflage fatigues, he was hiding behind a log in a patch of tall grass watching an enemy strong point, a Vietnamese village, as he waited for a high-ranking Cong leader to keep an appointment.

The mental battle was the same—a fight against fear and frustration brought on by weariness. The physical fight was the same—battle the enemy and win, no matter what the odds, no matter how vicious the opposition. He had to endure, and at the same time, as a man, he had to try to understand the *why* of it. And through it all came the primary, the most important factor: in order to fight and to win he first had to survive.

The Executioner knew about surviving—he had lived through a long war against the Mafia; now in the new war against terrorism he had spent another lifetime charging into unthinkable odds. There were new wars to come, as Bolan's personal ability to act in battle came up against the restraints, even possible betrayal, of the labyrinthine organizations that purported to work in their nation's defense. But Bolan would win, if he kept his wits about him at all times, undistracted by any but the most loyal and battle-hardened allies. Bolan would win because he was not only a survival specialist—he was also a death-bringer.

Lying against the hard surface of the valley between the holds on board the *Contessa*, Bolan pushed such thoughts out of his mind.

The closest double-rotor bird had landed fifty yards away, and sat roughly the same distance from the elevator on the far side.

Firepower. Bolan needed a rocket launcher and six rounds.

Bolan checked the AK-47 automatic rifle he had taken from the dead man on the steps. It had a full magazine. He decided it was time to go public with his position. The Executioner lifted the Russian rifle and sighted in on the closest chopper. The pilot's side door opened and a figure exited.

The rifle spoke sharply with a 5-round burst and the pilot was jolted away from the aircraft. He dropped to the deck. At once a machine gun opened fire from the chopper's side door. The rounds slammed dangerously close to Bolan. He ducked below the hold cover and rushed ten feet closer to the bird. He rose and sent six rounds into the cockpit of the helicopter, hoping for a hit on some vital instrument cluster.

A machine-gun round splattered against the steel only three feet from him. Tiny bits of lead dug into his shoulder. He crawled a dozen feet farther along the depression. He sighted over the pipes and emptied the rest of the AK-47's 30-round magazine into the open door of the chopper. The enemy fire cut off at once.

Bolan discarded the empty rifle and ran bent over to stay below the pipes. As he moved toward the chopper he saw that the angle would take him within twenty yards of the aircraft. He hoped they were short on guards around the chopper.

For a moment there were no shots, no roaring aircraft engines, just the soft breeze off the sea. Even the silence seemed threatening. Sharp pain from the minor shrapnel broke through the anesthetic of his combat adrenaline. Flecks of blood from the surface punctures and grazes soaked into the fabric around them. Nothing serious—so far. Bolan checked the magazine in the Beretta, pulled it out and put in a special 60-round magazine he had been saving in the pack. The Beretta manufacturers had recently built a few according to specifications from Andrzej Konzaki, Bolan's weaponsmith.

He moved more cautiously. His combat senses froze him in his place, the silenced Beretta up, waiting, the fire selector on three shots.

Ahead a foot scuffed along waterproofed metal.

Bolan held his breath, waiting.

Another step sounded.

He slowly pulled a throwing knife from a scabbard on his right leg, held the Beretta in his left hand, fingers on the sensitive trigger, and waited. He cocked his right hand over his right shoulder, gripping the stilettolike blade with his thumb and three fingers.

He was ready.

Another scrape of a boot. The nightfighter's cold

blue eyes stared into the blackness. At last he saw a dark shadow move, then move again, black on black.

Bolan waited. His hand was motionless.

No moonlight shone from above. Threatening clouds now covered the sky.

He waited another second.

Then he saw it, the white smudge of a face in the inky space before him. Target acquisition: directly below the smudge.

The blade flew from his fingers, and a second later a surprised grunt was followed by a long, low rasping whisper and the gushing of the dead man's last breath.

As the body fell, a gun clattered into the troughlike gutter between the holds. Bolan sprinted the dozen feet to the corpse, picked up his rifle, another AK-47, and checked the man's pockets where he found three more 30-round magazines.

Bolan collected his war booty and hurried down the trench. Three guards paced nervously around the chopper just at the edge of the floodlights. The body of the pilot had been removed. One dead pilot did not kill the bird. Undoubtedly there would be a backup pilot on every chopper.

The large cargo doors gaped open. There was plenty of room inside to put one, two or maybe three of the fuel-rod lead caskets.

It fired his resolve. He could see the machine gun mounted just inside the cargo doors. It was unmanned. From his combat pack Bolan took out two WP grenades. The White Phosphorous was one of his favorite incendiary weapons. The chemical exploded out of the grenade, caught fire when it hit oxygen, and was impossible to extinguish.

The Executioner judged the distance to the chopper. Close to thirty yards. He was no major-league pitcher, and he could not risk a bobbled throw. He had to move closer. The guard nearest him had turned sideways, watching into the darkness. The sentry wore a paramilitary uniform, which meant he was a mercenary hired for the transport. Fine. He got his paycheck, he took his chances. The Executioner moved in.

He lifted the Beretta, rested it on the top of the hold cover and sighted in on the guard now fifteen yards away. The man turned and stared into the void toward Bolan.

The Beretta sneezed once, emitting a tiny shaft of flame near the muzzle of the silencer.

The mercenary guard took the round through his nose, into his brain where it stopped, mashing up half a dozen life-vital centers and ending a short and unproductive life. . . .

Bolan crawled on his belly, powering himself forward across the deck with his elbows and feet. He got to the edge of the light spill and realized he was visible. In one surging burst of energy, he stood and ran, darting the remaining distance toward the chopper.

He pulled the safety pin from the grenade and held the handle down.

He lobbed the white phosphorous bomb into the open door of the helicopter ten feet away, saw it bounce once and land in the cockpit.

He turned and charged back toward the friendly darkness. Twin shots followed his steps.

Then the soft *whump* of the exploding grenade came from behind him, and Bolan dived into the murk of the shadows beyond the body of the dead terrorist.

The Executioner rolled twice, felt bullets whipping around him, and then he was in the gully below the hold protectors.

Warily he peered over the top. The Willy Peter grenade had done its job. Smoke poured from the door of the bird. He could see flames eating away at the interior. A moment later he heard small-arms fire as ammunition inside the chopper exploded from the intense heat. Screams came from the other side of the flames.

One of the rockets on the fuselage exploded, then two more exploded and the whole deck area billowed in flames as the fuel tanks erupted with a thundering roar, raining aircraft parts down on an acre of decking.

Two down, two to go.

Bolan stared at the elevator for the first time since his blast there. The exterior door had been mangled. It had been pulled off and was lying to one side. The interior of the huge elevator seemed to be intact.

There was no one inside the elevator. As he watched, Bolan saw four guards walking back and forth in front of the lift. They were heavily armed with rifles, side arms and grenades. He would have a tough firefight going through them, and right now he could see no need to try. The other two choppers had to be the highest priority. Bolan could see them in their circles of light behind the elevator. One still bristled with weapons, the other seemed to be purely a cargo craft. He checked his weapons. He still had three phosphorous grenades, six frag grenades and two cubes of plastique in his pack. He also had the two 60-round magazines for the Beretta, and the AK-47 with four magazines. It would have to do.

A speaker nearby clicked on.

"Attention. Attention. Everyone listen. Our leader has something to say to you." The words came over the speaker in accented English.

"This is Captain Lutfi. This is a warning to all those who resist us on board the *Contessa*. We are in complete control here. We have the crew members as hostages. If there is any more resistance, any force used against our people *whatsoever*, I will order one of the hostages shot immediately. Any continued disturbances or weapons fire, or any resistance by the unauthorized persons now on board, will lead to another hostage being executed. These deaths will be on your head. I expect complete and unquestioned compliance with this order at once, or fatal results will quickly follow."

The Executioner stared into the darkness. His priority had just changed. He was going to get Lutfi.

The guy had to be in the radio room on the bridge deck to make the speech. Or did he? Where were his quarters? Bolan stopped his sudden rush of planning.

Was he letting the purpose of the announcement destroy his own strategy? Was his humane and automatic instinct to protect the innocents distorting his mission plans and tactics?

Bolan knew he was at war. In any war there were

casualties. Calculated risks had to be taken and losses expected.

The Executioner knew he was holding the life-death decision in his hands for one or possibly more of the hostages.

Now he thought through all sides of the problem. He knew what route he had to follow.

At all costs he had to prevent the loss of the fuel rods.

If one more crewman on the *Contessa* died, that would be a tragedy, true. But the larger tragedy would be if ten, twenty, perhaps 100 *million* innocent human beings died in an atomic catastrophe.

Mack Bolan carried the AK-47 and hurried through the series of valleys around the hold covers, working under and over the maze of pipes and walkways on the large deck.

Slowly he came closer and closer to the next helicopter that had to be destroyed.

His mind was made up. No innocents whatsoever would die.

12

Captain Hans Running stared across the small table in his private quarters at the man he despised from the moment he first talked with him on the radio.

"You will not kill any more of my crewmen," Captain Running said softly.

"And if I do?" Lutfi asked, sneering.

"Then surely you, too, will die. Only in wartime does our society grant man the power of life and death over any of his fellow men."

"Right," Lutfi agreed, "and I'm at war with ninety-five percent of the nations on this earth."

Hans Running scowled. He was fifty-two years old and had put in enough time to retire, but had not been able to deny himself the challenge of commanding the largest vessel afloat.

With today's tragedies he wished he had refused command.

However, during these past few hours he sensed that he had grown in understanding, in simple maturity, and with that feeling came an increased strength.

"No, Lutfi, you are not at war," he grunted. "You're simply an outlaw, a common low-class hoodlum. Society will not put up with what you are doing."

Lutfi ignored Running's comments. "You still haven't answered my question, Captain. Which crewman will be the next to die?"

"None of them—because the forces now on board the *Contessa* will soon have your pirates captured or killed and you will be forced to give up your dreams of grandeur. You are not a world leader. You are nothing but a common thief, robber, murderer and now a failed hijacker."

Lutfi smiled. "Thank you, Captain Running. You have just sealed your own fate. You have volunteered to be the next hostage executed. I'll have the word sent out over the ship's communication speakers. I'm proud of you, Captain. Frankly, I didn't think you had the guts to volunteer."

"I'll be alive twenty years after you're dead and forgotten, Lutfi. Your dream is shattered. You'll never get away with even one of the fuel rods. You know that if any of the fuel rods are moved without proper electronic coding, it will short out the mobile carts they ride on."

"It doesn't matter. We'll use your forklift trucks to move them. We've thought of *everything*, Captain."

"Except for the counterforce group now on board. I saw the leader. He's a big man, six foot three, two hundred pounds. And he had scary eyes. There was a lot of retribution in those eyes. He and his force will have you bottled up within half an hour."

"Not when we have twenty-nine hostages left," Lutfi laughed. "Shall we make a wager? No, you won't be here to pay me."

A speaker on the desk between them clicked on. A

voice in excited Italian spouted a sentence. Lutfi listened, gave a curt command, then snapped off the speaker.

"In case your Italian is weak, that was one of my men reporting that he now believes only one man is responsible for the problems we're having. He says we now have this invader under fire and that our sharpshooters will bring me his head in a bucket within five minutes."

"One man? You're being foolish, Lutfi. No one man could cause you all the losses you've encountered. Fifteen men killed, two helicopters destroyed. It's at least a ten-man squad of experts. I wouldn't plan on dinner if I were you."

"Rubbish. Five minutes and I'll be toasting my victory. If not, then in ten minutes I'll be marching you out on deck and my second-in-command will put a dozen rounds from an AK-47 rifle through your heart. And no one will weep for you."

The speaker came on again. The Italian words were sharp, excited. Sounds of small-arms fire could be heard.

"So, it won't be long," Lutfi said. "They are attacking this ten-man army of yours right now. Already your life is forfeited because of this fight. Soon we shall see if your death has been in vain. Even if the crazy man attacking us dies, you still die. I have given the men my word, and they will cheer as you fall."

13

The Executioner had been working his way aft on the tanker. He was trying to get into position to take out the next chopper, but four well-trained gunmen cut him off and pinned him down.

These were a different class of enemy than he had seen so far among the terrorists. They were quick, disciplined—they were soldiers.

For a moment he could only fire and fall back. He spent one of his frag grenades and threw them off the track. He already had the French gunship, piloted by Jack Grimaldi on the destroyer, ready to lift off, but that was his reserve. Only if worse came to worst, would he call in Grimaldi to give cover and more fire-power.

Bolan made a wide detour around the opposing riflemen. He figured they had out-flanking protection so he faded into the darkness and angled for the stairway door on the superstructure. If he could not get at the chopper, he would have to get Lutfi—and personally prevent the terrorist leading from making any more moves of death.

Most of the terrorist activity and personnel seemed to be near the elevators and the choppers. Bolan needed to examine the office area of the ship in order to locate Lutfi himself. He darted into the stairwell and ran quietly to the second floor, where he cracked open the door and looked into the hallway. Six doors led off it. He had to take a chance. Bolan ran into the corridor.

The first door was locked. Bolan bypassed it and checked the second. It was unlocked, but the room empty. The third door on the same side of the hall opened into a bomb factory.

The Executioner stepped inside and let go of the door, which swung shut automatically. The latch clicked. The lights in the room snapped out, leaving Bolan in coalmine-at-midnight blackness.

A wild heartbeat later the combatman heard a snap, then a soft laugh. A recording. The laugh turned into a strident voice. Lutfi's voice.

"So, the rat fell into my trap. It's good to have you here. Do be careful moving about. The room is filled with small- and large-charge explosive devices, all set for hair triggering in the most ingenious ways. And all of the bombs will detonate at once if you attempt to force open the door. Now that we understand each other, I'll turn on the lights."

The lights came on, fluorescent, recessed under heavy plastic shields in the ceiling.

"As you must have guessed," intoned the bodiless voice, "this is a recording set to activate as soon as someone entered the room. A little game I play. Oh, yes, I have failed to tell you the rest of the rules. There is a time limit. You have exactly one hour in which to unravel the puzzle to all of the twelve explosive devices. Any not defused after an hour will automatically detonate.

"The room? Not to worry. This room is specially built to withstand and contain the explosions. Unfortunately, no human can stand such forces.

"One more suggestion. These devices are all wired and constructed differently. It's a hobby of mine and I'm extremely good at it. There are make-to-break detonators, there are break-to-make types, and there are some that explode if they are moved vertically, some if moved horizontally. There's one that must even be kept absolutely level. And, of course, you know about the big one already activated by the timer. So good luck."

The recording had ended.

Bolan made a cautious inspection of the room. Lutfi was, of course, right; there was no way out. The walls were solid.

The bombs all used various amounts of C-4 plastique for the explosive. He stared at the closest one. It blinked with red and green lights that had no pattern. The next one had a beep that sounded each two seconds, then varied and after an interval repeated some pattern sound.

The Executioner knew a lot about explosives, but he was not a bomb expert. If only Gary Manning, of Bolan's Phoenix Force, were here right now! Just one wrong wire pulled and any one of these bombs could go off, creating a disastrous sympathetic explosion with the rest of the C-4.

Bolan looked around, saw a chair and was about to sit on it when he stopped, knees bent.

He knelt and looked closer at the chair. There was a pressure-sensitive device on the seat, and under it a square of explosive. If he had sat down, it would have been the end of the war.

Mack Bolan stood still, staring at everything in the room. Everything—the chair, desk, picture on the wall, the small sink and mirror—could be booby-trapped.

No doubt bombs were indeed a hobby of the terrorist, but one point in the recorded message did not ring true.

Lutfi had been on board the *Contessa* less than twelve hours. He could not have constructed this room in that time. The room could not essentially be any different from the others on this deck. All had the same construction.

Bolan walked carefully to the closet wall, the one shared with the vacant room he had just looked at. He found no booby traps on the floor. The wall looked natural enough, no pictures, no signs. Just a plain, painted surface. He touched it, then gambled, tapping it gently.

Solid, but nothing happened, no explosion, no alarm. The booby trapper had not wired everything. Bolan pulled the heavy K-Bar knife from its scabbard and touched the point to the wall. He twisted. It did not dig a hole. No luck that it could be drywall. Cautiously he scraped some of the thick paint off the wall. A shiny metal surface showed through.

Metal, but how thick was it?

The Executioner placed the point of the K-Bar against the metal, waist high. Gripping the knife tightly, he thrust forward with all of his 200 pounds of power. The heavy, flue-flame-tempered stainless-steel blade penetrated and sank inward a quarter inch. He lunged again, and the knife sliced through the thin aluminum alloy, all the way to the hilt.

Bolan withdrew the blade halfway with a scraping sound, then forced it downward, slicing through the metal. He remembered doing the same thing with a pocket knife on a can of beans. Almost any knife could cut thin metal with the right force, although thicker metal required tremendous force from a very, very fit man. Bolan pushed the K-Bar down again and it sliced a foot before it stopped. Now he pried back the metal.

Inside he found insulation, and beyond that another thin metal covering.

Five minutes later he had sliced open a small part of his side of the metal wall, pulled out the insulation and cut through the other metal wall.

Another five minutes and he had carved a hole big enough to crawl through. He was out of the bomb room and into a vacant room.

He walked to the door, opened it slightly and stared up and down the hallway. No one was there. Just before he stepped out, he heard the ship's intercom system come on.

"Punishment call! A dozen hands are ordered to report to hold fifteen, directly beside the superstructure, for a discipline call! You have five minutes. Captain Hans Running will be our star pupil for this exercise. Don't miss it!"

Bolan recognized the same voice he had heard on the tape: Lutfi. He had spoken English in this new announcement deliberately. The Executioner slung the AK-47 over his shoulder and prowled back the way he had come.

He did not know where hold fifteen was, but he knew he had to find it fast—Captain Running's life could be at stake. Bolan melted into the darkness under the eight-and-ten-inch-diameter loading pipes and listened. He checked his watch, then squatted on the pebble-rough surface of the gully between the holds. The tough metal surface offered good footing and was painted a dull black.

A moment later he heard voices. Bolan stood on the hold cover and looked for the meeting site. As he did, a floodlight snapped on.

Bolan sprinted silently down the gully between the hold covers. He unslung the Russian rifle, checked the magazine. One more intersection down and he came to a spot where he could see the group and have a good field of fire. Ten men had gathered under the light. Standing on top of the hatch cover with his hands behind his back was Hans Running. Two riflemen jumped up on the cover and stood at attention twenty feet away.

Lutfi's voice babbled rhetoric over a bull horn.

The two riflemen brought up their weapons. As they did so, Bolan fired once, moved his aim and blasted again, both single shots critically aimed.

The first round caught the firing-squad man in the center of his chest, blowing him backward off the hatch. The second bored a round hole through the other rifleman's head.

"Captain—this way!" Bolan shouted as he sent a dozen rounds over the heads of the men who had come to witness an execution. They scattered. There were a few return rounds, but the gunners had no target. Captain Running dropped into the gully between holds, scurried into the maze of pipes, valves and walkways, and was quickly hidden from his searchers.

Bolan met Running at the valley two holds over.

"You might need this," Bolan offered.

"They'll come after us," Running said, panting from his run.

"They won't even get close. Besides, they have a more pressing job. And who knows this ship better than you do? Is there anything we can do to disable the elevator they bring up the fuel rods on?"

Captain Running shook his head. "Not without blowing out the power in that section. Then the whole nuclear plant could go down."

"How many men does Lutfi have left?"

"No more than twenty, counting the men from the choppers that just came in. You did all this by yourself, didn't you? All this hell?"

"How many fuel rods can be taken out in one chopper?" Bolan asked.

"We never haul more tnan two, but he might try three."

"Can you use this?" Bolan tossed the AK-47 at Running in the best army tradition.

Running caught it with both hands.

"Sure. I was a squad leader in the Korean War

before I joined the Merchant Marine, about a million years ago. . . .''

"Good. You know your ship. How can we get close enough to those two undamaged choppers to kill them?''

The Captain nodded, motioned and ran. Bolan followed. Minutes later they bellied up behind a pile of equipment on one of the hold covers. Thirty yards beyond them sat the next chopper. This was as close as they could get.

The deck between them and the aircraft was table flat, and without a pipe or winch or building.

"We take out this one, then move on to the gunship," Bolan said.

Captain Running nodded in agreement.

Bolan drew his AutoMag and sighted in on the cockpit for his first shot. He fired and saw the heavy slug plow through the cockpit. But before he could sight in again, a chattering barrage of fire came back. Bolan and Running slid into the gully as the hot lead continued raking their position.

"They've got most of their defense force around that one ship," Bolan said over the gunfire.

Running put the rifle muzzle over the steel cover and slammed off five rounds, then jerked the weapon down as another heavy volley of small arms and machine-gun fire raked the steel top over their heads.

Bolan waved at Running, and they dashed thirty feet down the alley and peered over the black cover again. Now Bolan could spot the defenses. A systematic line of positions had been created in front of the chopper, using upright steel plates.

Bolan stared at the defenses for a moment and frowned. All he had to do was get through that wall of fire and burning lead and kill the big chopper. But how?

14

Bolan knew from its defenses that this chopper must be the key one, the transporter. He lifted the AutoMag and blasted at the helicopter again, but was driven down by a withering fire storm of small arms and machine rounds.

He and Captain Running hurried along the depression and under more pipes to another vantage spot. They looked over the top of the hold cover. They had moved far to one side of the chopper. Bolan now understood why Lutfi had put up such overwhelming, steel-plated protection: two moon-suited men walked beside a forklift truck that rolled slowly forward on the deck, carrying a coffinlike box on its forks. The crate was ten feet long and at least three feet square—an atomic-fuel-rod shipping coffin— sturdy, lead lined and fairly safe.

Bolan reached for the Captain's AK-47, put it on automatic fire and sent a sizzling firetrack at the moon men. He knocked the first guy down, but the rig rolled forward. A fresh volley of terrorist bullets drove the Executioner back into the steel gully.

Fire and move. Crouched over, Bolan ran, hidden in the depression, racing back to the chopper, the captain on his heels. Bolan stopped, checked his position, moved another ten yards and pulled two grenades from his pack, one a white phosphorous and the other a fragmentation. He judged the distance to be forty yards. Too damn far.

He pulled the pin on the white phosphorous and, using his strong right arm and all of his experience, hurled the small bomb toward the target.

It hit short, bounced on the hard landing pad and rolled, but was still well shy of the chopper when it exploded.

The sudden fire produced a white smoke that soon nearly hid the chopper. Bolan pulled the pin on the frag grenade and tried a different tactic, throwing a ground ball, trying for as much roll as possible.

But still it was too far. The grenade was rolling when it exploded near the metal bird. Rifle fire blazed through the grenade smoke, slamming into the metal over the hold cover.

Bolan gave the captain the Beretta and two magazines.

"Take this up there about fifty feet and give me some cover. Divert some of the fire your way. I want to pick off the driver on that forklift. No driver, no delivery."

The Captain ran. When Bolan heard the shutter of the little automatic pistol, he rose up and aimed his contribution of 7.62 whizzers from the AK-47 at the transport vehicle. He knocked the driver off the seat and the caravan stopped.

Seconds later, another driver climbed back on board, pushing a heavy steel plate in front of him. Round after round glanced off the steel.

The Executioner tried to shoot out the tires, but the slashing lead had no effect. The rig kept moving. The tires were probably made of solid rubber and could soak up a thousand rounds.

A moment later the slow-moving forklift worked behind the steel shields with their riflemen protection force, and Bolan lost his target. He could not even get a clear shot at the chopper. For a good field of fire he needed to go to the other side.

There wasn't time.

He spotted another forklift advancing. This one came with a steel shell around the driver and no moon men. Unless he could get a lucky shot at the engine, this load would get through to the chopper as well. When he looked at the fork lift again, he realized it was electrically powered—no engine to shoot out.

What he needed was some G-Force.

Bolan unclipped a small powerful radio transceiver from its case on his web belt. He whispered into the built-in mike and speaker.

"Stony Man One to G-Force."

There was a five-second delay. Bolan could picture Jack Grimaldi reaching for the transmit button as he came out of a deep concentration.

The familiar voice came softly from the small speaker with a tin-can sound.

"G-Force here. That's a go."

"The game's getting serious "

"Give me some numbers and I'm over there."

"Can you give me an ETA of five minutes?"

"You want it, you got it. When?"

"Soon. I'm shy on firepower. We've got two birds here playing truck, hot-cargo type."

"Use me, or work too hard yourself!"

Bolan grinned. "That's a roger. I'll be on the forward half of this big island when you come in. The two whirlybirds are aft near the superstructure under spotlights. I'm moving around the ship like it's Death Star—there are gullies everywhere and I'm using them to stay out of sight and to keep moving at all times. This is one weird battle."

"Save some fun for me," the air jockey said.

"Plenty here to go around. Stay hard."

"You got it. G-Force on standby."

Bolan turned off the tiny transceiver and put it back in the pocket on his webbing, then trotted toward where Captain Running should be. There was no sign of the sailor. Bolan kept moving. He still wanted to check the far side of the birds—put one of them out of commission with rifle fire. He had three AK-47 magazines, or ninety rounds left. And Running had the Beretta.

Each time the nightfighter made a turn and peered up to check his progress, the choppers were not any closer. It was like walking through a maze at midnight. Finally he lifted up, spotted them and moved closer. Now he could see the terrorists were loading another lead coffin into the second bird. He sent a 10-round burst at the loaders, but could not tell if he did any damage.

He wanted to blast away, to take advantage of the crazy geography of the ship that allowed so many men so little chance of finding the source of the sniper fire that hounded them from constantly changing positions. But from his present angle and range, he could not hit any vital spots on the chopper. Besides, now he had to start counting rounds.

He ran again, along the sunken gully, hoping to get a better spot with a good field of fire. The Executioner passed near the rail on this surge and for a moment he stopped. He heard a strange sound, a throbbing, a gushing. Bolan ran to a deserted part of the rail and looked overboard. He cursed silently.

Even in the darkness he could see it—a long, shiny slick extending away from the tanker.

He could hear it and smell it, a flow of oil being pumped from the tanker, splashing into the sea.

Lutfi was a man who wanted to leave his mark on the world, even if it was only a 1,000-mile oil slick across some of the most fashionable and expensive beaches in Europe.

Bolan stood in the pitch darkness at the rail, the automatic rifle hanging toward the deck, his face dark with rage. For a moment he felt totally frustrated, useless. There was nothing he could do to stop the oil spill.

Through the night air the nearby speaker bellowed out its message.

"To the Western world. You have broken your promise to me. You have chosen to fight me, to send a combat force on board my ship. They have been met and defeated. All are now dead. My program is on schedule. You must furnish the gold by dawn. Even now I am releasing 10,000 barrels of crude into the sea. You will see it easily by dawn.

I'm told it should be on the beaches for a thousand miles along this northern rim of the Mediterranean. Congratulations. You have brought this event down on your own stupid heads. It is all your doing. It will be you who must answer. I wait for the gold, and the release of my fellow crusaders. Long live those who struggle against all of our foes!''

The speaker cut off and Bolan stared at the black sea again, then turned and hurried back into the network of gullies that cut across the huge deck. There was nothing he could do about the oil. But he could make Lutfi pay. And he could stop those choppers from taking off. That was vital.

Bolan reached for his radio and contacted Grimaldi.

"G-Force, your powder dry?"

"Ready when you are, Sarge."

"It's a go. Give you five minutes ETA. We have the same two birds still on the aft deck. I'd like you to greet them with some machine-gun fire and prevent them from getting airborne."

"Full bore? Rockets, the works?"

"That's a negative, G-Force. Negative. We can't risk damaging the cargo in the choppers. Your machine guns should handle the job. Keep both birds down and dirty."

"Splash them easy, that's a roger. Keep your ears on."

"Yeah, and keep 'em flying, G-Force. Out."

Bolan turned up the volume on the small radio and slid it into a slit pocket on his right shoulder. He could hear it and talk by hitting the send button with his left hand.

The Executioner ran to the rail and looked over. Now he could hear more pumps working, gushing more crude into the sea. One way or another Lutfi was going to leave his mark. Mack Bolan was *dead certain* of that, and before this night was over, Lutfi would be the same way. *Dead. . .for certain.*

15

When the Executioner turned to scan the strange, checkerboard deck of the *Contessa* in sniper style, he saw a figure slipping in and out of the shadows, working toward him.

Bolan jerked up the AK-47, but before he found the target again, a voice filtered through the soft Mediterranean night.

"Captain Running here. No sweat, GI. I'm on your side."

Bolan lowered the weapon. "Thought I'd lost you. What happened?"

"Doing some recon. I'm using the gullies for hide and seek. I had no idea they'd be so useful! The terrorists have three of the fuel rods loaded in one chopper and one in the next bird. But we can take one last try to knock them down."

"You know this ship, what's the play?"

"A fire hose."

"Fire hose? We tell them to stop shooting while we sprinkle them?"

"Almost," smiled the captain, keeping his voice low. "We're set up with a complete fire-fighting system, mainly foam cannons that can be aimed from positions every fifty feet along the center walkway. But we've also got a little gadget that has tracks on it, a kind of mobile water cannon. We can hook it up to the high-pressure water. Have you ever been hit by a high-pressure stream of water from a water cannon? It's like getting slugged with a sledgehammer.''

"Against machine guns?" Bolan said.

"If we can surprise them. That way we wash half their defenses down the deck and have a chance to move in on one of the birds. We've never used this mobile fire cannon, but it gets tested regularly. It's a hundred yards back in that little utility barn. We'd have a straight shot at that first chopper.''

The big guy nodded. "Then let's go for it.''

They jogged into the tight jungle of the ship, along deep trenches free of mud or predator, through the complex metal branchwork of pipes and cables that had never seen wild creatures but now knew sniper fire as if the ship was a part of Nam itself. Then they cut toward the distant one-story building that paralleled a mass of unloading pipes and tried the door. Unlocked. Running opened it and they looked at the water cannon rig.

It was six feet square, covered with a plastic tarp. It had crawler tracks at the side, and a four-inch-wide nozzle mounted in the center, with what looked like stabilizing feet that would prevent the rig from tipping over when the water-shooting started.

"She has an electric-drive motor, quiet as a cat. We can hook into the high-pressure water line a hundred feet from that first chopper. She's electronically controlled from this portable console. All radio directed, of course.''

''Lead the way,'' Bolan said.

Captain Running turned on the device and worked the control panel, guiding the crawler out the door. It moved along, silent on its soft treads, toward the target.

They detoured around splashes of light from the floods, and three minutes later they were in position. The two men set up near the unloading pipes, just behind a steel walkway. The walkway would give them ample protection.

The water cannon was a hundred feet from the chopper. Captain Running quickly connected four-inch-wide water hose to the cannon and to the shipboard pressure system.

He held up his thumb. ''Hooked up and ready to go. We've got 100 feet of hose if we need it. That gives us some maneuvering room. It's made to withstand 800 degree heat.''

Bolan had been looking at the control panel. He moved the levers and the small tanklike device crawled ahead, then stopped. They had a straight shot down the deck toward the chopper.

''Get down and stay ready with that AK-47,'' Bolan said. ''Things are going to heat up in a rush.''

He moved the little tank forward. When the liquid cannon was fifty feet from the chopper, somebody shouted. Bolan nodded at Running who turned the valve, and the water jetted into the hose. The rig stopped, self-activated its stabilization extension feet on all four sides and locked onto the deck.

A small green light glowed on the Executioner's control module and he flipped a switch. Now he could direct the nozzle. He made some adjustments and hit another switch.

A powerful jet of water fifty feet long arced toward the chopper.

Bolan moved the control handle, and the solid shaft of water shifted lower and blasted a terrorist gunner off his feet, sending him sprawling downstream.

Bolan lifted the stream, pouring it into the open cargo door of the bird. Then he moved on to the front door, blasting the heavy stream at the cockpit.

He washed down four more guard posts, then aimed the stream back at the cockpit.

Gunfire erupted, the rounds aimed at the cannon, but there was little of the tank that was vulnerable. The heavy metal turned aside the puny lead rounds.

The Executioner jetted the water against the aircraft. The rotors began to turn.

Desperately he aimed the water directly on the rotors, trying to deflect or unbalance them, but it did not work. They turned faster and faster. He put the stream back at the cargo doors, but they had been slammed shut. The cockpit became his target again, then two riflemen. He washed the gunners away, but the glass would not yield.

Slowly the big chopper began to inch off the deck, lifting higher over the light standards.

Captain Running lifted the AK-47 and emptied the

magazine into the bird. He jammed another 30-rounder in, but by then the chopper was gone.

The small-arms fire was coming deathly close. Both men tumbled into the life-saving ravine between the big holds. Bolan scurried down twenty yards and looked over the lip. To his surprise, he saw that the chopper had landed a hundred yards farther aft. The pilot must be waiting for the second craft to be loaded.

Sudden lights along the rail grabbed Bolan's attention. He looked closely and saw two crewmen with flaming torches. The men threw the torches over the side.

Captain Running had handed the AK-47 back to Bolan, who now lifted the weapon and sent three quick shots at the half-shadowed fire throwers.

"The oil," Bolan shouted. "They're trying to set the oil slick on fire."

In the dim light he could see a crewman emptying a five-gallon can of liquid over the side. Bolan wondered what the liquid was—probably something more volatile than crude oil. *Gasoline.* Gasoline and the torches would ignite in hell fire.

Bolan aimed the AK-47 at the terrorist.

They saw the light blossom like a sudden morning sun over the side of the tanker. It seemed that half of the sea had exploded into fire.

"My God," Captain Running shouted, and turned toward the bridge. "I've got to move her. I've got to get the *Contessa* away from those flames, or this could be the biggest bonfire the world has ever seen."

Backlit by the flames at sea, a figure leaned over

the rail. Bolan could hear him laugh. The Executioner aimed the AK-47 and sent a sizzling firetrack of five rounds at the terrorist. The rounds slammed him over the rail. The Executioner heard only the start of the terrorist's death wail as he fell into the inferno.

Before Bolan could turn, they were in a firefight. Hot lead slammed into the steel covers, bounced off the metal and sang away into the distance. Bolan dived to the deck and pulled Captain Running down. He pointed toward the center of the blackness under the maze of pipes, and they crawled for fifty feet, slid around a corner in the gully and sat up.

Captain Running held his shoulder. Bolan could see a dark stain on the front where a slug had exited.

The Executioner examined the wound in the darkness. Even through the torn jacket he could tell it was much more than a simple scratch. Bolan pulled a folded square of bandage from one of his slit pockets and pressed the cloth over the wound inside the captain's shirt.

"Hold it there, tight. And stay right there. I'll draw them off the other way. They won't have time to come back for you. There are reinforcements coming in any second now. Keep your head down and the pressure on that wound."

Bolan watched Running for a moment, deciding the captain would stay put. "Where are they holding your crew?" he asked.

"Third floor in the superstructure," the captain replied. "Locked in. Don't get them killed."

"We need them to move this island if they can."
Bolan gave the captain the captured .38 revolver and
retrieved his Beretta. The nightfighter filtered away
into the darkness.

The numbers were falling fast. Grimaldi was on
the way. One of the choppers was fully loaded,
another one almost.

Bolan took the AK and his Beretta and bent over
as he ran down the gully and back toward the
enemy. He fired a 5-round burst, then cut down a
side ravine. He leaned over the hold and fired again.
The Executioner saw some answering flashes as
he worked back toward the birds. They would be
expecting him now, but he had to move that way.
He looked at the scene of the first burned-out chopper.

A voice cut into the night.

"G-Force, looking for Stony Man One."

Bolan touched the small-transceiver send button
through his skintight shirt.

"Yeah, G-Force. Waiting. What's your ETA?"

"If you're anywhere near that fireball on the water
up there, I'm about thirty seconds out."

"That's us. You'll see two choppers warming up
on deck, back toward the tall tail end of this thing,
near the superstructure. It'd be a hell of a big help if
you could kill one of them, but no heavy stuff. Both
those birds have fuel rods in them already, so play it
gently."

"Roger, I'll take out the first one I see."

A chattering of automatic rifle fire cut the conver-
sation short as Bolan dived below the lip of the

crease. He charged along the safety zone heading toward the stairway in the superstructure. He had to free the crew so that they could move the tanker away from the fire.

Bolan made one more circular dash, going around a gunman to the stairway door. A heavyset, nervous guard stood there, his rifle up and ready.

16

Out of endings come beginnings. It happens, Jack Grimaldi knew. He had seen fresh new leaves struggling out of the black rot of decaying stumps—new generations feeding off ancestors. That was nature's way. With people, nature sometimes needed a boost, someone to grease the skids from ending to beginning.

In Jack Grimaldi's case the boost was there when needed.

The old life had ended for Jack Grimaldi in a mob seaplane he had piloted to Puerto Rico, carrying an arch enemy of Grimaldi's employers—and, ostensibly, an enemy of Grimaldi himself—plus an accountant with a bagful of his employers' money.

That was a whole era ago and that enemy was Mack Bolan, the man called the Executioner, the man who for years had waged knowing war against Grimaldi's Mafia employers.

There were many things, though, that Mack Bolan did not know. Not then. He did not know that Jack Grimaldi worked for the Mafia only on a contract basis, flying the headcocks around the world in a variety of aircraft. He did not know that Grimaldi had previously flown a hundred thirty-seven combat missions in Vietnam, that he was highly decorated and twice wounded, that he had come home to a country weary of a no-win war and embarrassed by its returning veterans. He did not know that the Mafia flyboy job was the only employment Grimaldi could find that came near to matching his training and capabilities.

The Executioner did not know that the pilot lived only for flying, that it had been that way since Jack, at sixteen, had built and flown his own plane. He did not know that Grimaldi had begun to hate his life, that he didn't give a damn for the Mafia, didn't give a damn about what it was doing to him and everyone else in the world.

But Mack Bolan *did* know that Jack Grimaldi was flying him into a trap.

The whole episode was a tense, and largely unwritten, piece of modern history. . . .

As the seaplane had glided on its pontoons toward the trap, Mack Bolan had nestled the Beretta Brigadier he used back then against the flyboy's throat, and said, "End of game, Grimaldi. When the engine dies, you die."

That was when Grimaldi suddenly did give a damn. He did not want to die. Bolan had it wrong. . . . He wasn't a Mafia headcock, not even a hardman. He wasn't Bolan's enemy. . . .

And yet he was leading Bolan into a trap. Why? Because there was an enormous reward on the Executioner's head. Grimaldi wanted that reward. It was the pay dirt he'd been looking for all his life.

Grimaldi never flattered himself that he'd talked

Bolan out of pulling that trigger. But Bolan had not pulled it. Twice more, Bolan had had his chance to kill Grimaldi, but did not do so. Was it merely that he needed the pilot's services? Perhaps. Was it more? Had Bolan seen in Grimaldi a potential ally? Had he seen in Grimaldi the aura of sadness that surrounds warriors returning from a useless war?

Or had Bolan seen something even deeper? Had he known that, by sparing Grimaldi, he was creating a new life, a life of meaning, one in which Jack Grimaldi no longer would not give a damn?

Whatever the case, Grimaldi knew, it had happened. He left his old life there in Puerto Rico, like a decaying stump. He rose from that stump, like fresh struggling leaves, and became something he'd not even aspired to before.

He became Mack Bolan's ally. For the next eight years, he fed Bolan information about the Mafia and helped Bolan in a number of raging wars against his employers. In Texas. In Seattle. In Tennessee. In New Mexico. In Florida. In Baltimore.

Grimaldi had been there, flying and fighting, during the Executioner's final week of intense warfare against the Mafia. He'd been there at the ending of Mack Bolan's old life and the beginning of his new one.

And *that* ending and beginning had made its indelible mark on Jack Grimaldi. He ended yet another phase of his own life.

He quit the Mafia and lived to tell about it.

Always new beginnings from old endings.

It never concerned Jack Grimaldi that he was to be

the backup man. If people said he was playing second fiddle to the Striker, hell, he'd love it. Second fiddle to a guy like that was a giant leap forward for any man.

As for Bolan's intense hatred for Animal Man that preyed on the gentle people of the earth, well, Grimaldi hadn't given it much thought before that day in the seaplane. But in the decade since, he'd given it a lot of thought.

For Sergeant Mack Bolan it had begun when his father was driven to desperation by Mafia loan-sharks, had killed Bolan's mother and sister, had wounded his kid brother, Johnny, and had taken his own life. But that tragic event alone did not sustain the blitz artist for a whole decade. What sustained him was an awareness that a whole new war was being waged on the home front, that he had the skills to engage in that war, to *become* that war.

Now, Bolan, as Colonel John Phoenix, had a new life—he had been made chief of the Sensitive Operations Groups to be known as "Stony Man."

Slightly miffed that he'd been left out of the colonel's first big battle—in Colombia—Grimaldi had taken off in his rebuilt, refurbished and highly-cherished F86D1 "Saber Dog" Saber jet. Ostensibly, he was going to Costa Rica, where there were rumblings of a new problem involving missing F-104 Starfighters. But the problem could wait. Grimaldi, after marking time, went streaking after Mack Bolan, the colonel, the "Sarge," against all orders.

He arrived in time to pluck his mentor from a wind- and battleswept Colombian hilltop after a hurricane had closed down all escape.

And he found a bonus. The colonel had a new convert in tow, a battle-hardened, highly skilled and very beautiful lady terrorist named Soraya. Grimaldi had a weakness for women; he always had. Soraya was not just any woman. She was—well, he had to find out. After accepting criticism for his disobedience, and praise for his nick-of-time rescue, he took Soraya along on the other problem.

Costa Rica was quiet. He found nothing. Oh, he found out about Soraya.... And then came the message from Stony Man, from Hal Brognola. The terrorist wars were on. He was needed full time. It was a new beginning.

He remembered then that hollow feeling when he'd gone into his first solo takeoff roll, as a young man and had looked at that empty instructor's seat.

He had that hollow feeling right now, in the Mediterranean, ready to go to war once again with Bolan, ready to go to war against a truly crude killer.

17

The Executioner blew the guy away on the run with one carefully placed AK-47 head shot. The sentry's body slumped against the door and Bolan had to push the corpse aside.

He ran up the stairs to the third floor. He met no one on the steps and looked past the door cautiously. One guard down the hall turned and brought up a rifle.

Bolan removed him from the human race with a silent 3-round burst from the Beretta, then ran to the second door on the left. Locked. He shot the lock twice with the Beretta and kicked open the door.

Fifteen men poured out. Graciously they thanked the man who helped them escape captivity. Bolan nodded, then fired instructions. "Oil is being pumped out. We've got to stop the pumps. And the sea is blazing with burning oil. Move this ship away from that fire. Now."

They all ran for the stairs. Bolan opened the second door, released the rest of the crew and told them the same thing. They hurried away and Bolan followed. As he stopped to pick up two full magazines from the dead guard at the door he heard the chatter of machine-gun fire coming from the sky.

Jack Grimaldi in his borrowed French attack chopper slammed in from the left.

Bolan watched the chopper, its motor wide open as the attacking bird flew down in a diving strafing run.

Grimaldi must have thought he was flying a fully armored Tomcat fighter aircraft, the way he zeroed in on the grounded chopper and blazed away at it with his fixed twin machine guns!

The G-Force man had attacked so suddenly that there was little return fire, even from the guards around the chopper. Grimaldi and his French bird flashed past them, then ducked below the deck of the high ship, swinging away from the target before the gunners could sight in.

On deck the enemy chopper took dozens of direct hits from the machine-gun rounds. Bolan watched as the lead messengers burned lines along the body of the craft, then raked over the cockpit.

Grimaldi came toward the chopper again, aiming first at the small-arms fire that blinked at him from the deck, scattering the opposition, then he spun around and strafed the big chopper.

Bolan hit the talk switch on the transceiver under his shoulder.

"Nice shooting, G-Force."

Even as he said it he heard a *whup-whup-whup* from somewhere ahead of him on the other side of the big tanker.

"G-Force. Can you see the other bird?"

"Negative. I saw it on the first pass, but it's gone now. Must have lifted off into the darkness."

"Alert all our radar in the area. We need to watch for her. We must have some kind of a heading."

"Right, they're watching. Now for some more target practice."

Grimaldi completed the third run on the chopper. This time he concentrated on the helicopter's cockpit.

The Plexiglas went first. Immediately a small fire started. By the time Grimaldi wheeled away and broke off his attack, the big bird had slumped on one side and her slowly spinning rotor grazed the deck, breaking one blade off.

"Splash one, G-Force. Does that bus pick up passengers?"

"Only if you got the fare."

"Come in on the starboard side toward the bow, away from those guns. I'll get up there so you can see where I am. We still have some angry shooters down here, so watch your tail."

"Got it, Stony Man."

Bolan studied the big ship. He had a quarter-mile run through enemy troops.

An automatic rifle stuttered behind him, chipping paint from the steel beside his head. The big man surged up and ran down the depression toward the middle of the ship, where Grimaldi could land without taking too much small-arms fire.

The mission was not yet half done. One more chopper to find, and one mad terrorist to locate. Not half over.

18

A rifle bullet slammed past Bolan as he ran forward. From the other side of the ship, an automatic weapon chattered sudden death at him, but missed. For a few seconds he could not turn either way. He had to bore straight ahead, away from the protection of the loading pipes and the steel walkway on top and the valleys between the holds.

A shadow moved ahead of him, and he fired three rounds from the Beretta 93-R he held in his right hand. The shadow screamed and fell backward.

Behind Bolan an explosion ripped through a second-floor room, blasting furniture through the wall, billowing with red and black smoke.

The bomb room was potent after all! And it had triggered at least fifteen minutes early.

When the resounding slap of the explosion slammed past, the nightfighter saw a section between the holds and darted into it. He ran hard toward the center of the ship.

A burst of fire forced him back toward the area where the chopper lay dead, tilted to one side. They were trying to herd him. He paused at another junction of the holds and checked over his shoulder. He could see no one in pursuit. Twenty yards ahead stood the wounded chopper, and just beyond that was the forklift truck the terrorists had used. He heard sounds behind him, took a grenade, yanked out the safety pin and threw the bomb. Bolan darted toward the forklift. The grenade explosion seemed louder than usual because all other firing had stopped. The quiet continued.

He sprinted past the bird and jumped on board the steel-plate-protected forklift truck. No key was needed. He switched on the electric engine, put a lever in 'forward' and the rig responded.

A rifle slug bounded off the metal plate. Then another hit it, and he felt a third slam into the sheet metal of the small tractor. But he kept moving. He rumbled across the pad and up the side of the tanker free of loading pipes, and on toward the far bow of the ship. Bolan heard a chopper pass overhead and hit his small-transceiver talk button just as another pair of rounds careened off the metal sides.

"G-Force?"

"Got you."

"See the moving forklift? That's me. Anywhere you can set down, I'll be a paying passenger."

"I'm looking. Yeah. A spot a hundred feet ahead of you near the rail. Flat. See you there."

The chopper hummed in close, its machine gun beating a tatoo at someone behind Bolan. Then Grimaldi was overhead and soon touched down.

The Executioner piloted the forklift as close as he could get, felt three more rounds *spang* off the metal protectors, and then bailed out, darting in a zigzag toward the French chopper. He jumped in and slammed the door. An inch from his face a round hole appeared in the aluminum metal. The chopper jolted into the air. Another round hit the Plexiglas window and glanced away. Before Bolan could find his seat belt, two more rounds zapped through the cockpit.

The chopper tilted away from the ship and slanted downward toward the waves until it was less than ten feet off the dark water as it raced away from the huge tanker. A few farewell shots blinked from the *Contessa*, then they were out of range and away. Clean.

"Thanks," Bolan said.

"Like driving a bus," Grimaldi cracked.

"Any compass bearing on that other bird?"

"Sketchy, but the military boys have a radar track. As far as they can tell, the heading will take that hot bird over a small island about twenty miles to the northwest and about a mile off the French coast."

"That could be it," Bolan grunted. "Can we find the spot?"

The French chopper had more speed than Bolan figured. He knew the other bird was heavily loaded.

The radio chattered. A voice reported that radar had spotted the enemy helicopter again. It was still on the same course. French aircraft would be rising to meet it.

"No," Bolan barked into his mike. "No military planes of any kind in that area. I want one target out there, not a batch of friendlies shooting at each other. No military air in that area. Make everyone understand that. And I want an assault force to hit the *Contessa* and mop up the mess there, got it? Make it a French force.''

The U.S. destroyer commander took the message without comment.

They flew for ten minutes.

''Something coming up on the screen,'' Grimaldi said.

''Moving?''

''No, it must be the island. Now if the damn clouds will stay away from the moon for a few minutes.''

The small island materialized ahead of them from the soft night sea mist. It was little more than a high sandbar with a few trees and one small hill. On the far side of the five-acre plot of land huddled the dark forms of two buildings. Winking lights came from below and Grimaldi jolted the bird to avoid ground fire.

''Somebody down there doesn't like us,'' the pilot said.

''Yeah, but who is it—our hot-cargo chopper?''

They made a quick pass, coming up low from the water to check out the building. Bolan fired the AK-47 out the side door as they slammed past. Partly hidden by a tarp, a helicopter sat beside the cinder-block building.

''That's as close as we're going to get to a positive ID on them,'' Bolan said. ''It looked like the same chopper to me. Let's make a strafing run.''

Grimaldi nodded. The ex-Mafia pilot hovered the craft 400 yards away and poured machine-gun fire into the chopper. The hot lead sliced through tarp and found metal.

Grimaldi swung the chopper out and came back at a different angle and slanted his double machine-gun fire into the chopper once more.

After a third hosing down of the area, Bolan spoke. "Let's take a look."

They came in slowly, at a hundred feet, ready to cut to either side. As they flew closer they could see the riddled canvas.

A sudden flash exploded below them.

"Watch it!" shouted Bolan.

The minisecond Jack Grimaldi caught the flash, his finely honed reflexes slammed the chopper downward and to the right, away from the trajectory of whatever fired.

"What the hell was that?" Grimaldi asked.

By that time the fiery trail of a rocket tore through the sky above and to the left, exactly where they had been a second before.

"Some kind of a hand-held rocket launcher," Bolan said. "Maybe an old 2.2. or 3.5 bazooka—but when that round hits you, it doesn't matter what tube it came from."

"I suppose you want to go down and mop up and check for radiation," Grimaldi said.

"Got to. Only way we'll know if it's the right chopper. Put me down at the far end of the place so I can sweep it as I go."

They landed in the darkness on a sand spit two hundred yards from the downed chopper.

Bolan stepped out and Grimaldi was right behind him, pulling the lever, charging an Ingram submachine gun without a silencer. The pilot extended the telescoping stock of the weapon and put three 36-round magazines in his jacket pockets. The magazines were loaded with the standard 9mm parabellum cartridges.

"This is a two-man job," the sky jockey said. "Like it or not—and I don't—I better give you some close support."

Bolan smiled. "Told you I'd make a foot slogger out of you yet. We must make sure they're terrorists before we shoot. If they blaze away at us, they're fair game. There could be some civilians on this island."

The slab of land was a hundred yards wide, so they spread thirty yards apart and went down the middle in the moonlight, clearing any possible hiding spot by autofire as they moved. Bushy grass covered the island's far end, which meant there was no place to hide. Fifty yards ahead was a growth of stubby trees, twisted and battered by the strong sea wind, but still surviving.

The two warriors were halfway to the trees when rifles sounded. Both men hit the ground.

Bolan watched the fire for a moment. Two enemies, he decided. When the next burst came from the one on his side, Bolan sent three 5-round bursts from the AK-47 into the position.

Two minutes later there had been no more firing from Bolan's man, but Grimaldi's terrorist kept shooting. The Executioner sent five rounds into the other enemy spot, then surged up and charged twenty feet ahead and hit the dirt on knees and butt of his rifle before lying flat. Just as he hit the ground, a spatter of deadly whistlers parted the air over his body. He rolled five yards into a slight depression and waited.

Now would be a good time for Grimaldi to give him some covering fire.

From behind he heard the Ingram chattering, blasting out a stream of 9mm parabellums at 1200 rounds per minute.

Cover! Bolan leaped up and ran forward. He made it to the trees and flattened just inside the scrub growth. The moon was tagging the clouds again. He waited for a bright spot but could see nothing to his left. He moved at combat stalking speed, slow enough not to miss any danger, but fast enough to cover the ground before the quarry bugged out.

A cough came from the left. Bolan froze. The cough sounded again, strained. The combatman moved slowly, not disturbing a leaf, not breaking a twig. After ten feet, he looked around a small twisted pine. A man in jeans and a blue T-shirt lay on the ground, a rifle at his side. He had turned on his back and Bolan saw the blood on his chest. The terrorist moved, tried to rise, then flopped down. A rush of the last breath he would ever take whistled from his mouth.

Explosive automatic fire just ahead sent a dozen lead death-dealers screaming around Bolan, thudding into his protective tree, zinging past him. He slammed to the ground, his automatic AK up and ready, but he had no target. The Ingram screamed again, and Bolan edged forward toward the direction of the incoming fire. He took a frag grenade from his straps, pulled the pin and held the arming handle down in his right hand. Bolan put the AK-47 over his shoulder on the sling and carried the Beretta in his left hand.

The moonlight spilled down for only a few seconds between new cloud cover, and Bolan stared past the pine. Twenty feet ahead he saw a man in a blue-and-white shirt and camouflage pants working on a jammed automatic rifle. The combatman rolled a grenade toward the terrorist.

The rifleman, hearing a sound, looked up, his eyes wide with a fear visible even in the silvered darkness. He screamed just as the grenade detonated.

The terrorist's body lifted a foot in the air from the force of the explosion and the chunks of shrapnel slamming into it. The rag doll then tilted backward, blood pouring from a dozen deep wounds before it fell to the ground.

Silence flooded the end of the small island. Bolan cupped his hands around his mouth and called.

"That's a go, G-Force. Clear here."

"Thanks. You do good work."

Bolan waited a minute, saw Grimaldi edge from behind a pine tree thirty yards over, and waved. They moved forward.

There was no more opposition as they cleared the remaining hundred yards to the buildings. They had worked up with basic infantry tactics: one man advancing and covering the other. Now they lay in the short brush at the edge of the open space and looked at the chopper. The helicopter sat near the block building.

Bolan pulled out his Starlite Scope from his belt

pouch and studied the bird. He could see into the open cargo hatch. He could make out the long heavy caskets containing the fuel rods.

Bolan and Grimaldi lay there not making a sound. They watched and waited. The attacking force always has the advantage in a siege. The defenders must defend at every second, but the attackers can pick their time. A break came three minutes later when someone coughed inside the chopper. A whispered reprimand followed. Two terrorists in the bird, Bolan concluded.

Bolan had seen that the lead-encased fuel-rod caskets were strapped together with steel bands for security and protection. They would easily withstand a grenade blast. He pulled his last frag grenade from his pack.

"Going hard," Bolan whispered. He handed Grimaldi the grenade, indicating the chopper's open cargo hatch. Bolan sighted in with the silenced Beretta, folding down the front grip, putting his thumb through the enlarged trigger guard for a firm support.

He feather-touched the trigger for a 3-round burst. The chugging of the shots came through as distinct coughs. Grimaldi threw the grenade.

The three rounds drove through the terrorist's neck, pulverizing his spinal column, smashing his body back four feet.

Bolan and Grimaldi waited without moving. For five minutes they lay there in the sand watching, listening for any movement.

Bolan leaned over to his pilot, whispering so low the sound could not carry.

"I think our condition red is over. I'll check. Cover me."

The Executioner rose soundlessly, sprinted to the chopper's side and edged around to the cargo door. Big Thunder was out and in his hand as he checked the chopper's interior.

An animal cry pierced the silence. A terrorist dived at Bolan, thrusting a bayonet toward his chest.

Big Thunder bellowed twice, slanting 240 grains of hell-bent lead into the figure's belly and chest. The force of the .44-Magnum rounds stopped the terrorist, and he fell to the chopper floor, eyes glassy, the bayonet dropping from his hand.

The Executioner stormed through the rest of the chopper, clearing it. No one else on board was alive. He found another body behind one of the large lead-lined caskets. All three of the containers were intact.

Bolan jumped from the chopper and ran to the cinder-block building. The door was open. He charged inside and came out a minute later. It was an unused shell. No one was in either of the buildings; both had been empty for a long time.

He started out the door when he heard a burst of gunfire. He dropped to the sand and recognized the almost-continuous explosive sound of an Ingram firing 1200 rounds a minute. It had to be Jack. Bolan crawled to the corner of the building and found his pilot standing in the middle of the clearing, staring at a body at his feet. The terrorist lay in a death sprawl, a grenade—with the safety pin still in it—held in his hand.

Grimaldi glanced up at Bolan and pointed his eleven-and-a-half-inch chattergun at a trail.

"There were two of them sneaking up on you. The other one went up that trail. He was a little guy."

Bolan gave his buddy a nod of thanks. Then they ran into the brush, moving through the dark growth and watching the trail while making sure of each other's position. It took them ten minutes to work through the denser growth on the higher part of the small island.

They paused just below a slope that climbed fifty feet in twenty yards. The trees were taller here.

Only Bolan's keen observation for movement helped him spot the danger in time. There was no warning, only a quick three steps and then a killing lunge for the throat.

The steel-capped toe on Bolan's right boot had been aimed quickly at the leaping dog's head. But the canine's spring had more power and distance than the Executioner had estimated and his kick caught the dog in the chest just over his heart.

Bolan fell backward, and when he hit the ground he swung up the Beretta. But the dog was lying on its side, pawing the ground spasmodically. The German shepherd was at least 130 pounds. He was down and dazed but not injured. From a slit pocket, Bolan pulled some tape, and bound the animal's front legs together.

Grimaldi and Bolan worked up the hill again and, after five minutes of delicate maneuvering, looked through a screen of brush and small trees at a small tent. The Executioner crawled behind a thick log and stared over it.

He motioned Grimaldi down, then cupped his hands and shouted.

"You in the tent. You're surrounded. Come out with your hands up and you won't be killed."

For a moment there was no response. Bolan blasted three rounds from the assault rifle over the top of the tent.

Five seconds later the tent flap moved, then flipped back. A boy, about ten, draped with three automatic rifles, combat webbing, a dozen grenades and two pistols stepped from the tent. He held his hands high over his head. Nearly too late, Bolan saw the grenade hidden in one hand. The boy tossed the bomb at Bolan, and he heard the spoon *spang* away as it flipped off, arming the flesh-shredder.

Bolan dropped behind the log he was kneeling beside as the grenade went off harmlessly on the far side. The boy had fallen to the ground to protect himself. Grimaldi lifted from behind the log and grabbed the boy, who stood, glared at his captors and held on tightly to his weapons.

Bolan checked inside the tent.

"It's a damned arsenal in there," the Executioner said. "Probably fifty weapons and ammo all over the place."

Bolan taped the boy's hands behind his back.

"Keep an eye on this warrior here while I clear the rest of the island," he said to Grimaldi.

It was a short look. Twenty feet behind the tent the land dropped off in a cliff to small breakers below. He was out of island.

Bolan marched the young boy back to the clearing. They put him in the first building, taped his feet as well and told him someone would come along soon to help him.

"Americans, go to hell!" the boy spat at them. Those were the first words he had spoken. His English had a French accent.

"With the likes of you around, little warrior, we're already there," Bolan said.

He went to check the big lead-lined coffins in the dead chopper once more. There was no apparent major damage. The lead inside would stop any bullets, and the steel bands were firmly in place.

That took care of the stolen enriched uranium. Now, where the hell was Lutfi?

19

Jack Grimaldi eased the chopper away from the island. Bolan had instructed the French navy to send in two helicopters and ten men to secure the island until daylight. They would take care of the boy and the dog.

The assault force that Bolan had authorized to land in choppers on the flat bow of the *Contessa* had battled it out with the remaining terrorists. A 120-man force had been ready for ten hours, and it took off within two minutes after receiving Bolan's radio message.

Lutfi? Lutfi could not have hidden on that island, and he had not been found among the dead. No, Lutfi would play the odds. He knew the chopper would be tracked, followed by radar and captured. Lutfi was still on the tanker, waiting for his chance, trying to work his magic again, turn a disaster into a partial success.

And he still had the radio-activated detonator.

The French troops had secured the bow and the forward half of the tanker by the time Grimaldi brought his bird in for touchdown. The troops radioed that half the big ship was firmly in French hands and that they were moving toward the stern, clearing away any resistance as they found it. None of the troops had seen Lutfi.

When the Executioner stepped on the ship's deck, he knew her screws were turning. She was under way. They had come in upwind, and now Bolan could see the fire burning in what seemed to be half the whole sea behind the tanker. A crazy, useless fire, set by Lutfi in frustration and rage. Perhaps, at least, it would consume some of the oil before it despoiled the coast.

The Executioner took an English-speaking French paratrooper with him, and they trotted up to the advancing squads. The troops were meeting little resistance. Six terrorists had given up and were huddled together on deck with their hands tied behind their backs.

Captain Running staggered out of the darkness and was caught by a trooper. The French medics went to work on him quickly and stretcher-bearers raced up. Bolan knelt beside Captain Running.

"We're going to save this old tub of yours, Captain."

Running grimaced. "Lutfi. What about that damned radio-activated detonator?"

"I'm looking for him. So are a hundred twenty French troopers. Any idea where he'd go?"

"Below, I'm sure he's below somewhere. Tried to dump the rest of the crude when the last chopper left without him. My men stopped him, but he wounded two of them. We forced him out of the pump room and stopped the spill. I'm sure he's below."

From his study of the layout of the *Contessa*,

Bolan knew there were only a few areas where a person could go below; the engine room, storage areas, pumping rooms, generators, maybe the settling tanks, turbine rooms. . . .

Bolan ran for the elevator. He was ahead of the paratroopers now, and he warned them not to blast him, thinking he was a terrorist.

The Executioner was just past the burned-out chopper on the pad when a handgun barked. Bolan felt fire stab through his left shoulder. He dived to the deck and rolled behind the chopper's hulk. He tried to lift his arm.

Pain ripped through the wounded area.

But at least he could still move it. The slug had missed bone. He picked up the AK-47 rifle and found that his arm still functioned. He would ignore the bullet hole and the pain. He had to.

Something moved in the semidarkness ahead of him. He stared around the burned, twisted metal at a shadow. A 3-round burst from his Beretta brought a grunt of pain, then shuffling steps as the shadow moved quickly, retreating out of sight.

Lutfi. The man who shot him could be Lutfi. Bolan moved cautiously, listening to the slow progress of the other man. Then a sudden noise directly in front of him surged into his consciousness, but before it could register, a bellowing animal of a man burst out of the passageway, firing a weapon, knocking the Executioner to one side as he stormed past. Bolan did not even have time to raise his weapon. Lutfi again, doing the unexpected.

Bolan swore at himself. He was not hit. He came

up running, tracking the man through a maze of pipes, steps, ladders and off-loading equipment.

A barrage of small-weapons fire sounded behind them, then all was quiet. Bolan could see the man's goal: he was working his way toward the elevator near the forward side of the superstructure. There was no chance for a clean shot at the guy. He moved from one shadow to another, darting across open spaces, melting into blackness. Three times Bolan drilled 5-round bursts from the AK-47 at him, but none found flesh.

At the elevator, Bolan worked around to the front in time to see its lighted interior sinking below the deck line. He studied it a moment, then saw a steel emergency ladder extending downward into the dark hole. He slung the rifle, grabbed the rungs and began stepping down. He could see the top of the elevator still descending.

The elevator moved slowly, and Bolan got to the bottom of the shaft a few seconds after it landed. He stepped past the cables to a catwalk and looked out cautiously before he eased into the lighted passageway. It was part of a large white room.

The sound of running steps resounded down the corridor to his right. Bolan followed the sound quietly. The passageway made an abrupt turn and came to a double blast-proof door. The twelve-inch-thick barrier stood open two feet. Bolan bent, peered around it knee high, and saw a man down the passageway. The terrorist fired but Bolan had already jerked his head back and sent three rounds toward the guy

More footsteps. This time the terrorist disappeared around a second corner. Cautiously Bolan followed. There was no one in the next area, but he spotted an access door slightly ajar. He kicked it open and jumped back.

Two slugs blasted through the open panel and dug into the opposite wall. A laugh echoed from inside.

Bolan looked into the open door from one side and found only blackness. He kept low and squeezed through the hatchlike door. He was on some kind of a metal walkway.

When his eyes adjusted he saw it was a metal catwalk, with a single pipe railing on each side three-feet high. He could not see what was below or to the side. He wanted to use his pencil flash, but knew it would make an ideal target. Slow footsteps seemed to be sounding directly ahead. Bolan triggered a burst from the 93-R Beretta. There was no reaction. Bolan heard more footsteps, moving away from him.

The Executioner grabbed the railing, slung the AK-47, let the Beretta hang by its cord, and began walking across the metal bridge. He had no idea where the walk led. There was no light except that behind him at the door. There was no acrid smell of crude oil, either, which meant they were not walking across the top of one of the huge holds filled with oil. So where the hell were they?

This was not part of the atomic-engine area, or the reactor or the cooling apparatus. Bolan knew the general layout of such facilities and this did not match. He was in a black void.

Bolan stopped moving and held his breath. It was

totally quiet. Then ahead he heard a scraping of metal on metal. It started and stopped. It sounded as if one section of the metal walk were being removed.

Could Lutfi do that?

Remove part of the walk and invite Bolan to take a long step downward into death?

20

The sounds that had been coming from ahead of Mack Bolan through the blackness stopped. He eased forward, testing each step, making sure there was solid steel beneath his foot before he put his weight on it.

The routine slowed him.

Gradually he relaxed and became more sure of his position, knowing that Lutfi could not set up an elaborate trap for him in only seconds.

On the next step his foot brushed something. Bolan heard the *sprang*, that unique sound when a hand grenade spoon pops off, arming the device, granting the listener only 4.4 seconds of life.

Four and four-tenths seconds!

Bolan dropped on the bomb, finding it by the sound. He propelled it forward along the metal walkway with a scooping, shoveling throw, then he dived back so his boots faced the blast site.

The grenade went off with a jolting, mind-numbing roar, amplified a hundred times in the confined space.

Bolan shook his head, felt his boot soles and found only one small shard of shrapnel, otherwise he was untouched. He listened, but could hear nothing. His ears were numbed. The explosion had not been tightly contained and therefore lethally directed, but instead had diffused itself throughout the open spaces of the darkness here. Bolan's maneuver, dropping supine with feet facing the explosion, had saved many a combatman who found a grenade at too close quarters yet still had time to toss it horizontally into the open while lying back to let the shock waves and shrapnel fly over and around him.

He stood and moved forward, still testing each step, finding the metal welded and solid. Ahead there was nothing. It was black on black again. He moved, waited, moved, waited, but his ears still told him nothing.

Twice more he walked what he judged to be fifty feet and stopped. This time he could hear a clinking sound.

A second later, light flooded in as a door opened. Before Bolan could lift the Beretta, a shadow passed in front of the door and was gone. The Executioner rushed at the white light, sure that his prey's eyesight would be as shocked as his. The door was an oval hatch similar to those he had seen on the submarine. He ducked out and looked, then pulled back in. He had not seen anything. The glare, the unbearable brightness after total black still blinded him.

He tried it again and his vision had improved slightly. He glanced in both directions along a corridor. No Lutfi. At last his pupils had adjusted. Bolan held his breath, ears straining. Faint sounds came from the left. The guy was going back the way they had come. Something else caught Bolan's attention. On the white tile were drops of bright red blood.

Wounded. . . .

Bolan put a fresh magazine in the Beretta, a 20-rounder, and pushed a 30-round magazine in the AK-47, then followed the bloody trail.

He moved quickly along the corridor and paused at the corner to look around. Someone was closing a door ahead. It was the only door in the dead-end hall. Bolan ran to it, and standing close to the wall, reached out and tried the knob. It turned but the door did not open. Two rounds from his Beretta smashed the lock. Bolan stood to one side.

Five seconds later, three rounds from inside splintered out the door panel, chest high, in a neat pattern.

The Executioner faked a groan and stomped one foot as if he had fallen.

He waited.

Nothing happened.

Bolan twisted the handle, then jammed the door open. It swung wide inside and stayed there. At knee level he looked around the doorjamb.

It was some kind of control room, ten-feet square, filled with gleaming panels, gauges, dials and readouts. On the floor the Executioner saw three drops of blood. The last one was near the far door.

At that door, Bolan hesitated. Finally he turned the knob and pushed hard. The door swung away, and bounced back. Cautiously Bolan looked through a crack between the door and its jamb into another control room.

He saw a man in a white coat lying on the floor, a large pool of blood in a puddle around his head. A bloody footprint pointed toward the end of the room where a stainless-steel ladder led up one flight to a balcony that extended to the left and out of sight.

A voice stabbed through the distance.

"American! Why do you chase me? You know I can blow up this tanker any time I choose."

"You can, but you won't, Lutfi. You're not ready to commit suicide. Besides, you know one chopper got away with those fuel rods. You want to get to your meet so you can make your atomic bombs."

"That is true, American. And believe me, we will make them, and we will win. You capitalist whore, we will beat you in the last battle."

"Don't count on it, Lutfi. Your luck has changed, and you're leaking blood."

"I'm just getting started, American. You don't even know where I am. All I have to do is go through one of the six doors up here and you'll never see me again. This is a huge ship, American."

Bolan had been moving as the man talked. Already he was across the room and up the ladder to the lip of the balcony and had zeroed in on the voice.

He reached up and his Beretta coughed out a silenced trio of flesh rippers at the spot where the voice had been. Then three more.

There was no weapons response, only a soft laugh and the sound of a door closing.

Bolan vaulted over the edge of the balcony, the Beretta in front of him.

It was a trick. Lutfi stood twenty feet away, a

pistol in his hand firing as fast as he could pull the trigger.

Bolan's Beretta chattered twice as he lunged to one side, hit a railing and dropped to the floor behind a ledge to get out of the line of fire. One of the small-caliber slugs from Lutfi had creased the Executioner's left leg. By the time he got to his feet, the vermin had selected one of the six doors, slammed it shut behind him and rushed away.

Bolan knew he had been lucky. He never took any of his enemies lightly, but this one needed extra caution, special care and handling. Bolan knew he had come close to making that one fatal mistake that would forever end his war against terrorism. Mack Bolan knew he was human, fragile, expendable. He understood fully that one small quirk of fate one inch more this way or that with a smoking hot bullet, a thrown knife, a grenade fused too short, even a charge of plastique with a misfiring detonator, to say nothing of the countless persons who kept trying to kill him, and he would be listed simply as KIA. He had come to that realization many campaigns ago, but it was always good to remember, to know it was there without dwelling on it.

Bolan stared at the six doors. Identical. All were marked with plates: Fuel, Storage, Air Vents, Hot Side Cooling, Cold Side Cooling, Maintenance, in three languages.

He began at the end and opened each door, looking for telltale signs of blood. He found drops of red stain in three of them, but none farther along the corridors. Back at the balcony he checked the others.

Twenty feet along one hallway were more blood spots. It was his best indicator. This door had been marked Maintenance.

Bolan continued down the corridor to a series of downward steps, then to a vertical steel ladder. The ladder dropped into the depths of the ship. He figured he had come down fifty steps when he saw the landing and a room below.

The small room was marked with signs in three languages. The English one read:

Warning. This area for inspectors and qualified scuba personnel only. Breathing gear must be worn at all times when inspecting empty holds.

On the wall hung six sets of scuba gear—tanks, masks and air hoses. Bolan read the tank indicators. All were full. The set of gear from the first hook was missing.

Red lights glowed on the indicator board, meaning the oil storage tanks in that area were full. One had a green light with a lighted panel below that read Inspector Inside.

It had to be Lutfi.

Bolan pulled off a scuba harness, unslung his light pack and put on the tanks, then the face mask. He tested the air in the mouthpiece.

He walked down the narrowing corridor to the door with the green light over it. The same Inspector Inside sign appeared on the green panel. The small inspection door had information printed on it describing how the door automatically locked until the

level of the crude in the tank was below six inches.
Then it automatically unlocked.

Bolan saw that the door was only half open. As he
opened the door wider, he stayed behind it.

Instantly four shots sounded from inside the hold.
The slugs jolted against the inside of the door that
Bolan held.

The Executioner saw a light switch to his left and
flipped it off, darkening the dimly lighted inspection
room. Then, without a sound, he bent through the
opening, stepped inside and moved to his left. He
was blind for several seconds.

Then Bolan became accustomed to the dim light.
The room he was in was like a huge metal box, the
sides soaring upward fifty or sixty feet on all four
sides. He stood in six inches of crude oil, and now
realized he had not put on the special knee-high boots
he had seen outside.

Where was Lutfi?

Bolan breathed evenly from the scuba gear, which
he knew was needed because the petroleum would
vaporize and create a seriously unhealthy atmosphere
for human lungs.

A shot sounded in the gigantic echo chamber.
Bolan saw the flash to his right, but how far away he
could not say. He chose not to return the fire. It
would give away his position. The dim light made it
impossible to pick out a figure near the gunflash.

Bolan began working through the petroleum.

Moving was slow, like walking in two feet of
water. He concentrated on wading quietly.

He had sloshed a third of the way across the inside

of the tank when he heard a piercing laugh and the
sound of boots running on metal. Bolan looked up in
time to see Lutfi on a raised platform, running for
the door that Bolan had left open.

He saw a black form dive through the door into the
half light of the inspection room. The door clanged
shut, cutting off Lutfi's booming laugh and pitching
the tank into total blackness.

Without moving, Bolan concentrated on the spot
where he had last seen the outline of the door, then
began moving through the murk toward that spot.

He took his pencil flash from his blacksuit slit
pocket and snapped it on. It sent a strong beam of
light toward the door just ahead.

For two minutes Bolan studied the oval pressure
door. He knew it would have a safety device
somewhere. On a small panel to the left he found
printing etched on a copper plate, in three languages
again.

If you are inside when the door is closed: 1) Ring
the alarm bell. 2) Attempt to turn the emergency
inside wheel to open the door. 3) Use the secret
combination to set off the exploding bolts on the
pressure door.

Below that solution was a ten-button panel to
punch in the code.

He checked the inside wheel. At first it seemed
locked in place, but by exerting pressure on it, he
managed to turn the spoked metal wheel a few inches
at a time.

Ten minutes later the wheel spun easily and the door cracked open. The outside light was so bright it hurt Bolan's eyes. He pushed open the door and stood well to the side.

Nothing happened.

He looked into as much of the inspection room as he could. Lutfi was not there.

Bolan stepped out of the crude petroleum onto the metal floor and felt the oil squishing in his soft-soled boots. He cleared the area to make sure Lutfi was not there, then took off his footwear, stepped into some rubber boots and tucked his oily pant legs inside.

Ten minutes later he stepped onto the deck.

21

A French paratrooper challenged him. Bolan held up his empty hands.

"Hey, pal. I'm on your side," he said.

A curt command came from another voice, and the trooper lowered his automatic rifle and grinned. *"Ami?"*

"Yeah, buddy, I'm your friend, your *ami*."

A French officer ran up and saluted.

"Apologies, Colonel. All men do not know you." He spoke in English.

"Forget it. Lieutenant, did anyone else come out of this elevator before I did?"

"No, sir. No one."

"Thanks." Bolan looked at the ship and saw that four more military choppers had landed. Uniformed French troops were everywhere now. The situation seemed to be under control.

Except for Lutfi.

Except for the red holocaust box.

Bolan could see the flames of the sea fire a mile away now. Dawn was coming quickly. His shoulder ached where the bullet had hit him, but he drove the pain out of his mind. He looked back at the fire. Some multinational force was probably converging on the spill with all kinds of devices to soak it up, skim it, vacuum it, burn it off or use containment collars to keep it away from shore. He was glad someone else was handling that problem.

"Lieutenant Dupree," Bolan said, reading the soldier's name tag. "We're looking for a terrorist by the name of Lutfi. He's been wounded once, maybe twice. Last seen wearing a dark blue sweatshirt, green cap and light blue pants. He's six foot two and slight. Spread the word to watch for him. Dead or alive, lieutenant."

The Frenchman nodded, took a radio from his pocket and spoke quickly into it in his native tongue. The Executioner walked to the elevator.

At the elevator he picked up a phone that he had seen there before. It was answered at once.

"This is Colonel John Phoenix. Who is in charge of the *Contessa*?"

"The executive officer, Mr. Fisher."

"Put him on."

"He's extremely busy right now, sir and. . . ."

"Put him on the line at once!"

"Yes, sir."

A moment later an older voice responded.

"This is executive officer Fisher. What can I do for you, Colonel Phoenix?"

"Your man in the second control room is dead. Lutfi got him."

"We'll take care of the problem. Are the bombs still active?"

"Yes, until we find Lutfi and get that trigger. Where could he try to hide on board?"

"A hundred places. Everywhere but inside the oil tanks. He wouldn't live ten minutes in a full one or an empty one. But there are hundreds of other places. The French major says he has four bomb squads on board if we find the explosives."

"We'd better find them, Captain. We sure as hell better."

Bolan hung up and stared around the big ship again. Where would the Executioner hide on this tub if he didn't want 200 people to find him? The most unlikely spot. The place no one would think to look. Would not even check.

The empty oil holds, with scuba gear for breathing? Possible. Where else? He looked from end to end on the ship and scowled. Then slowly the idea came to him. He nodded, letting it build. Yeah, right. Where else? In an area no one would even suggest to search—in the radioactive fuel-rod storage area.

Perfect. One of those moon suits and Lutfi would be safe until the big search died down.

Bolan punched the elevator button that was marked Down. He had to find the white moon suits, get himself into one, and then figure out how to pull a trigger wearing those big gloves.

22

It took the Executioner only three minutes to retrace his steps down the elevator, through the corridors and past the control room where he found two technicians protected by a French paratrooper holding a submachine gun.

At the balcony with six doors, Bolan chose the one that was marked Fuel Storage.

The hallway turned once, then slanted down a ramp, but soon dropped sharply with a set of steps.

At the bottom of the steps he found a large room with a corridor leading off from it to the right. Ahead he saw movement, a moonsuited figure struggling with a helmet.

Bolan lifted the Beretta. The figure was thirty yards down the gleaming white corridor. The man in the moonsuit suddenly dived clumsily to one side, and vanished behind a dividing wall.

There was no protection in the corridor. Bolan hesitated. Then he charged ahead, the Beretta ready. He pounded hard down the tiled corridor and soon came to a large room with benches and lockers along the sides. On the doors were the words Radiation Protection Gear.

Bolan quickly cleared the room; Lutfi was not

there. A hallway leading away had been his escape route. Bolan wasted no time. He knew Lutfi was going into the fuel-rod storage areas.

He grabbed one of the suits from a locker and began getting into it. There were directions on the inside of the locker door. He felt the weight of the lead-lined cloth as he put on the pants and the jacket—the whole thing snapped and overlapped and zippered together for protection. He found boots and stuffed the bottoms of the pants deep into them as directed.

Then he put on the heavy gloves, but found there was no way he could pull a trigger without taking off one glove.

The helmet was the last item. The directions said someone should help him with it. But Bolan had no helper. He took off the gloves and at last got all the flaps, snaps and double protective shields in place. He stared out the small helmet window of lead crystal glass.

He walked down the hall, the Beretta in his ungloved hand.

It took a lot of effort just to move. The first sign he saw read Fuel Rod Storage and had an arrow pointing ahead. Around the sign were three radiation warning symbols.

The next sign read: "Has your Radiation Suit been checked at Inspection Station One?" Mack walked on, watching for hiding spots where Lutfi might be lurking. There were none.

The double doors he came to next were heavy, lead-lined he was sure. He pushed through them and found himself in another hallway of the same type.

Radiation detectors hung on the wall. He took one and ran it over the floor, picking up traces on the readout pointer. He passed it over his boots and found double the floor contamination. He held the probe to his luminous-dial wristwatch and got the same reading as on his boots. Not enough to worry about.

So far, so safe.

A short way forward he found two branch routes. One led to the reactor reloading center, and the second to fuel storage. He turned right toward storage. Over his shoulder Bolan carried the AK-47. He was not sure how he could use it, but he wanted to have all his weapons.

Twenty feet down the hall he came to another massive door. On the front in two-foot-high letters was the word, STOP!

Smaller printing read: "No one may enter without double-checked, double-protection radiation gear in place."

There was a button to push for admittance. He pressed it and a red light came on, followed by a recorded voice. "Sign in with your name and badge number, then place your right hand on the fingerprint identification pad for confirmation."

Bolan shrugged, put his bare right hand on the plate and the light turned green. Then he saw that the heavy door had not been completely closed and latched. He pushed open the door and stepped inside. Lutfi must already be there.

Ahead he saw a dozen cubicles, each with walls six feet high, each wide enough to hold a lead-lined coffin loaded on board an electric cart. All the carts seemed to be in normal positions. With the lead-shielding precautions, this work appeared to be as safe as being an attendant in a nursery. No radiation could leak from the caskets, and if it did, it would not penetrate the lead-shielded clothing.

Bolan took slow steps along the row of electric carts in their cubicles, but saw nothing unusual.

Then near the end he found one cart farther forward than the others, its front poking out slightly from between the high cubicle walls. As he neared it, the rig sprang to life and charged toward him, its electric motor on full power.

Bolan lifted the Beretta and fired one shot. The round hit the casket. Then he saw the moon-suited figure driving the cart. Bolan fired again, the slug slamming into the chest of the figure, but the lead-protective clothing easily stopped the 9mm round and the cart stormed ahead.

It was too late for a head shot. Bolan could tell that the driver's helmet was merely sitting on his head, not snapped and zippered and fastened on correctly. But by that time he had to try to dodge, to leap to one side. But the moon suit would not let him move that quickly—he stumbled and fell, the stock of the rifle going down beside his right leg.

Bolan had fallen in the path of the accelerating cart.

The cart's left rubber wheel hit his right shoulder first, pushing him forward even before its other front tire connected with his groin.

The impact was absorbed by Bolan's bulky suit, but the weight of the cart was crushing, almost unbearable.

A combat trick as old as time: in face-to-face unarmed engagement, let your adversary strike first! Whoever strikes first loses, for a moment, all the best possibilities of furious impact. For the person struck is the one who rebounds with the greater strength. The person struck is the one whose foulest temper is suddenly, instinctively, uncontrollably unleashed to wipe out the opposition.

So it was with Bolan now. Far from knocking him out of commission, the blow from the cart that rose up over him triggered all his rage in one explosive reaction.

Bolan lifted his heavily padded shoulder as the front end of Lutfi's cart rolled across his body.

It was an all-or-nothing uplift that mocked mere mortal strength. His fury sent the cart careening on two wheels, off in the direction of the wall across from the cubicles.

The action had saved Bolan's midsection from being sliced by the whole cart's weight on its two lower wheels, for by the time his surge was complete the cart was almost airborne. The moon suit was a fit adversary of the cart, for it was designed to resist powerful forces. But Bolan, the breathing biological form within it, one arm already punctured by a slug, felt nothing but a single wave of pain rolling back and forth through his body. As usual, the pain would not slow him, would not even be truly felt until the mission was over and the nerve-endings' complaints heard at last.

The cart swerved on for a full fifteen feet, tilted and out of control, building speed all the time. It slammed against the far wall and tipped over. The casket was dumped on its side.

The moon-suited driver lay crushed between the overturned car and the bottom half of the lead-lined coffin. Bolan could not see the fuel rod itself; it lay somewhere behind the life-giving shield of the lead coffin bottom.

Bolan ducked in behind the closest lead casket, wondering if it would provide any protection against massive radiation that must be coming from the opened coffin. He put his glove back on, awkwardly palming the Beretta.

Bolan heard mumbled words and realized for the first time that there was a minicommunication system in the moon-suit helmet. He spoke and it sounded strange.

"Lutfi. Can you move?"

There was a long pause. The mumbling stopped. "You're the devil, American. The devil."

The voice sounded eerie, hideous.

"Can you move? Can I get you out of there?"

"Why, American? So you can kill me slowly? So you can put me on trial and watch me die by hanging or firing squad? No thank you."

As Bolan watched, bare arms and hands reached over the top of the lead casket.

"American, I still have the small red box and its doomsday button. With a million and a half tons of crude oil, I can yet make the world's largest bonfire. It will be the most spectacular suicide ever recorded—mine! I'll go down in history for this—and we'll both go out in flames.''

"No way, Lutfi. Who will ever know? I'm the only one who knows you're even down here. No one will record it. You'll be swept like dust into a crack of history and be forgotten.''

"No. Someone must know. These little radios. They must broadcast to the bridge at least.''

"If they do, we'll be hearing from someone up there soon.''

"I *will* go down in history, pathetic American! I staged this whole tanker hijacking. I will foul 10,000 miles of beaches all over the Mediterranean. The world will remember me!''

"Forget being remembered, Lutfi. Why don't you *live*? Push the red box away from your position. Then I'll go for help. We'll get specialists in here who know how to rescue you from radiation exposure.''

For the first time Bolan saw a head lift over the edge of the coffin. The suit helmet was torn. The Executioner could see most of Lutfi's face. It was tinged a ghastly gray.

Lutfi's words came through Bolan's helmet. "At least I will not die alone. You will go with me.'' He paused. When the voice came back it was softer, weaker.

"I was married, did I tell you? I was married.'' Lutfi paused again. He was deathly sick. "She left me. Took our two children and left me.''

"You can find your children, Lutfi,'' Bolan said into his helmet mike. "They are older now and will have minds of their own. They will want to see you.

A man should always know his children when they become adults.''

"No, no, no," gasped Lutfi's voice. "I will never see them again, because I am going to die, here, today. You and I and everyone on this boat will die as soon as I close the switch and push the red button. All die . . . all die. . . ."

"Where are your children now? How old are they?" Bolan asked the fast-fading terrorist.

"They are in Roma. They are fourteen and fifteen, both fine boys. But I'll never see them again."

"Of course you will. I'll help you find them. We'll go together, next week. I'll talk to your wife and you will see your children. She must let you see them. I'll insist."

Lutfi's voice was barely a whisper now through the headset. "She'll never let me see them."

Lutfi lifted his hands higher over the edge of the casket. His right hand held a red box no larger than two packs of cigarettes.

Bolan sighted in with the Beretta, his ungloved finger on the trigger.

He fired.

Bolan knew he had scored a hit. He saw the slug strike the plastic, blast it out of Lutfi's feeble grip and then disintegrate the plastic and the electronic parts inside it, destroying forever the box's radio-sending ability. Even though its signals would never have penetrated the lead-lined walls of this part of the ship, the box's very existence had been a ticking bomb. Now it ticked no more. Bolan jammed his hand back inside the protective glove.

Lutfi could not feel his numb hand. He hadn't been able to feel anything for five minutes. He stared at the last bit of the lead shield that had protected his head and torso from the direct power of the fuel rod. The American had tricked him. It did not matter now. Nothing mattered.

He tried to lift himself up. He got halfway up, then fell, his arms outstretched, first touching, then wrapping around the lethal enriched-uranium fuel rod itself. He pulled his body on top of it. Lutfi gave a strangled cry and surged forward, hugging the metal container. And Lutfi at last found his endless, dreamless sleep.

Bolan had no first-hand experience of what direct massive radiation would do to a body. But he had no desire to find out.

He abandoned the unused rifle, then looked at the position of the opened lead casket. The protective bottom was toward him. If he crawled past it toward the door, he should be safe.

His route would keep him at least twenty feet from the back of the casket, and he was betting his life that he would thereby avoid any massive dose of radiation from direct rays. He had no other choice.

The Executioner moved, crawling on his hands and knees in the massive suit, making slow time, moving ponderously.

When he made it past the danger spot, he got to his feet and stumbled toward the door. Once outside the heavy door he slammed it shut. He leaned against it and breathed deeply.

With massive physical effort, Mack Bolan shuffled

back to the suiting-up room, located a phone and called the bridge. There was a nasty clean-up to do in the fuel-rod storage area that needed some professional, high-level attention. The Executioner did not want the job.

He did have one more clean-up job to do himself. . . in Paris.

23

The sun was coming up when Bolan walked out the elevator to the *Contessa*'s main deck. He stretched and blinked. The American Navy corpsman at his side had been judiciously careful not to touch him or assist him. But there was deep concern in the young man's eyes. Bolan brushed it aside.

"I told you, I feel fine. Your tests down there showed that I received only trace amounts of radiation on my right hand. So it peels or maybe I get a little blister. Don't worry about it. I'll bill Uncle Sam."

"Yes, sir. Whatever you say."

The man remained at Bolan's side.

"Your boss tell you to stick to me like a second skin?"

"Yes, sir. He isn't sure how much of the tests to believe."

"I won't keel over on you. I promise." He stared at the corpsman. "Lutfi, he was dead?"

"Lord, yes! He was little more than a crisp skeleton when our moon suits got to him. I've never seen anything like it. He was so radioactive they sealed him in a lead barrel. Burial will be in some 15-mile-deep sea trench, I'd guess."

"Fair enough. He wanted to go out spectacularly."

Bolan sighed. "Now, would you really like to help me?"

The youth nodded.

"Find the mess shack on this tub and roust me out a quart vacuum bottle of coffee. Hot as hell and just as black. I'll be around."

"Yes, sir!" the sailor came to attention, then hurried away.

It took Bolan another half hour to check with Lieutenant Fisher, the acting captain. The French bomb squad had found and defused the twelve bombs that had been expertly placed. If triggered, they would have split the tanker into four parts and at least half the crude would have been dumped into the Mediterranean.

Bolan checked out with the French major in charge of the troops, then sat on a hold cover to watch the French brigade mount their choppers and fly out.

Grimaldi found him there ten minutes later drinking coffee.

"You were looking for me?" Jack asked, a twinkle in his eye.

"About to. We still have transport?"

"The bus is ready and waiting, and only two bullet holes in her. Them kooks were lousy shots."

IT WAS JUST AFTER LUNCH that same day when Mack Bolan left Grimaldi talking to the French military about ways to improve their attack choppers. They had landed in the Tomcat and had taken care of the niceties with the U.S. diplomats in Paris. Now the Executioner had one last Parisian loose end to tie up—the end of the pipeline, the end of the site and the end of the people who were going to build the atomic bombs for Lutfi.

He rented a small car and headed for the address he had secured earlier. It was not easy to find. After making three fractured French inquiries, Bolan arrived at the right area. It was far north of Paris, in a rural place sprinkled with a few country estates, horse-breeding farms and the occasional cluster of houses.

The address he sought turned out to be at the end of a long lane off a country road. He spotted monitoring cameras at the lane gate. Strange, having a security monitoring system on an innocent country lane leading to three buildings that looked like they might be a small dairy operation. . . .

Bolan drove on, parked the car on a side road in some woods. When dusk fell, he changed into his black nightfighter's suit. He put Big Thunder on his hip and carried the Beretta 93-R on the lanyard around his neck.

With his other surprises and his web-belt gear, he was ready.

He jogged through the dusk, and came in behind the buildings. Two cars in the drive had not moved since he first saw them. Another rig came in and shut down its lights. Someone got out and went into the main building that looked like a farmhouse.

Bolan settled in a patch of willow near a stream 300 yards from the house and took out the Scope from his belt pouch.

The glow that he looked through showed that the

place was an armed camp. He could see a guard standing in a specially protected sentry post near the front of the first building on the lane. There was a metal gate on the road, evidently electrically controlled. He spotted three interior guards, two walking posts around the buildings, and one coming in and out of the main building, checking with the roving patrols. A regular little fortress.

The building the guards seemed most concerned about was the one that looked like a barn. Through the Scope, Bolan could see it had been extensively modernized. That would be his first recon target.

He moved when the guards did, working softly forward, taking advantage of the meandering creek until he was fifty yards from the barn. He glided in behind the building just as the guard completed his circuit and passed around the corner.

There was no door in back and the windows had been boarded up. Access was from the front or sides. He watched the guards. They were not paramilitary; they were poorly trained, inattentive, sloppy.

Bolan moved up and the next time the guard made his circuit of the barn, he shot him in the shoulder with one silent round from the machine pistol, then jumped in front of him and slammed Big Thunder down on the side of his head, knocking him unconscious.

Bolan dragged the guard back to the creek, took off his jacket and hat, donned them himself, and tied the terrorist securely. Then he picked up the guard's rifle and walked around the building twice. The other guards did not pay any attention to him. The third time around he slipped into the unlocked front barn door.

The building was a clean laboratory, filled with scientific instruments and long tables that looked as though they could be for some kind of assembly. A bomb factory? Bolan worked quickly, pulling quarter pounds of plastique from his pockets and planting half of the packages in four different places. He set timers on the devices for five minutes, then left. He walked his route once more and went to the building that looked like a farmhouse.

He went into a kitchen and heard voices in the next room. Someone was using half French and half English. Bolan could follow only part of it.

The important elements seemed to be that they had been listening to a television news story about Lutfi's attempt to get 400 million in gold by hijacking the tanker. Nothing was said on the news about the fuel rods.

A gangling youth of about twenty entered the kitchen. He stared into Big Thunder's monster muzzle. His eyes went wide. Before he could yell, Bolan hit him with his fist and knocked him down. When he opened his eyes the .44 AutoMag was touching his mouth.

"Stay alive," Bolan whispered. "How many in there?"

The youth's eyes went wide and he passed out. Bolan stood and looked into the other room. It was a living room. One man sat with his back to Bolan as he stared at the TV set. An older man sat in the next chair pulling on a bottle of red wine.

Bolan casually walked into the room, put the muzzle of Big Thunder against the partly bald head of the closest man and glared at the other one.

"Don't move."

The man in the far chair froze, the wine bottle still on his lips. Below the .44 a voice spoke that was vaguely familiar.

"Ah, yes. I was wondering when you would get here. You really weren't interested in my men's clothes store at all, were you?"

The man turned slowly and nodded at Bolan, then stood

The man was the small balding store owner from London who fronted the Lutfi bomb factory.

The Executioner centered Big Thunder on the Englishman's chest. "I should have known you'd be in on the payoff for Lutfi's work. Your supply has been short-circuited. Just as the TV told you—no Lutfi, no fuel rods, no enriched uranium."

"A pity," the Englishman shrugged.

They stared at each other for a moment.

"That oversized cannon is a waste of time," the Englishman said. "You'll never get out alive."

"Fine. Neither will you. Who paid for all of this?"

"Lutfi, me—a split, of course."

There was a knock at the door.

"Hold it," Bolan said. "Anybody comes in and you get two chunks of lead through your heart."

The Englishman sucked on his pipe, then nodded. "Yes, I believe you would do it." He raised his voice to the door. "Sorry, old chap, but we're busy now! Give us about fifteen minutes."

Bolan knew he had less than a minute to get away from the barn before it blew. Even here was too close for the amount of C-4 he had used.

"Out," Bolan said softly to the two men. "That way." He pointed toward a door. It led into a ground-floor bedroom. Bolan told one of the men to open the window, jump out and stand still. The older man did. Then the Englishman went through the window and looked at Bolan. The barn was on the far side of the house. The Executioner vaulted out the window, grabbed the leader by the arm and ran with him toward the blackness outside the ring of floodlights that had snapped on, leaving the older man behind. It was the Englishman that Bolan wanted to keep for questioning. The big .44 was in the back of the Englishman's neck.

"Remember if there's any killing, you die first," Bolan muttered.

The top half of the world exploded in one brilliant blood-red ball of fire and flame. The concussion knocked Bolan and the Englishman into the dirt and weeds.

As he tumbled to the plowed ground, Bolan saw the Englishman drawing a weapon from an ankle holster. But the Executioner was falling in the opposite direction to the Englishman's aim. By the time Bolan rolled once and turned, he saw the flash of the other weapon firing.

Bolan triggered twice, his strong right wrist and arm concentrating on holding the recoil action down for the second round.

The explosion in the barn continued rolling

thunderously. Bolan saw that the enemy's shot at him had missed. But Bolan's had not. The Englishman was coiled into a ball with his head flopping grotesquely backward. Brains leaked down his neck, their moistness reflecting the distant lights.

24

Mack Bolan stretched out on the red-and-blue striped blanket and felt gentle hands guide his head into a soft lap. He looked up at luminous eyes. April Rose's silky auburn hair framed her face.

"You've been a thousand miles away," she said. "Way out there." She dropped a ripe olive in his mouth. "I was wondering if you'd ever come back."

He sat up beside the tall, strikingly built woman and kissed her lips gently.

"Two slightly burned hot dogs coming up." He poked at the remains of the small fire he'd built in a ring of rocks near the stream that rippled through the meadow on Stony Man Farm. They had driven the Lazer Wagon off the trail and along the meadow to the very edge of the woods and found a perfect picnic spot fifty yards into the wooded area along the small stream.

And it was secure.

Here the Executioner could relax for a few hours. He pushed broken dry branches on the coals, blew on them and soon had a small blaze going. It burned down to coals in a few minutes, and by then he had the willow shoots ready, one for each hot dog. He turned the weiners and soon they cracked and dripped juices into the spitting coals.

"How's your shoulder?" she asked.

He flexed the left arm, winced and nodded. "Coming along. These hot dogs are either going to turn black or the sticks will burn off. Which way do you want yours?"

She smiled. She brought two plastic plates to capture the splitting franks.

"Time for one small wrap-up on the tanker affair?" she asked.

He nodded as he slid the hot dogs off the sticks.

"The French authorities found quite a bit of radioactive contamination at the remains of the French dairy farm. They estimate the workers there were about halfway through with the production of a series of atomic-bomb parts. All they needed was more enriched uranium. They've cleaned up the area, arrested eight people and found a few dead bodies in the rubble."

"The Englishman?"

"His name was Spencer Whitecliff-Jones. He's been in and out of trouble in Great Britain for years. Apparently he tied up with Lutfi two years ago. The whole atomic terrorism scheme seemed to be Whitecliff-Jones's idea. He did the planning, laid out the island base and the Paris country place as well."

"The French boy on the island?"

"Nobody knows anything about him or his dog. He's about twelve, a drifter who'd been living on the island by himself before Whitecliff-Jones came and made him a watchman."

Bolan slid the hot dog into a bun, smothered it with mustard and chomped off a bite.

"The oil slick," he said finally. "What happened to it?"

"The wind shifted, so most of it was contained in the clean-up collars, and a lot burned off. Less than five hundred feet of the French shoreline were touched by any oil. It was one of the biggest spills on record, and the quickest to be picked up and detoxified. Eight different countries sent equipment."

She touched his shoulder where the bandage was, her fingers light, softly trying to accept some of the hurt as her own.

"Captain Running is fine," she said. "The bullet wound was serious, but he should be back on duty in a month. The *Contessa* suffered a lot of damage, but she's covered by insurance. The fuel rods were all recovered, replaced in their usual positions, and no major problems seem to exist on the tanker. Was the ship really that big, a half mile long?"

"Largest in the world. Another hot dog?"

She shook her head. Her eyes followed his every move.

He looked at the water. "You ever do any fly fishing?"

She said she never had. She knelt beside him and put her arms around him, holding him tightly.

"You're not going to have any time to fish right now." Color splashed her pretty face as she unbuttoned the fasteners on her white blouse and shed it gracefully, like a beautiful flower opening to the sun.

He sensed his own swift reaction, warm, insistent, in total agreement.

They made love softly, gently on the blanket by the stream, totally free and giving. It was a long moment for themselves in the midst of global conflict.

Don Pendleton on
MACK BOLAN

Crude Kill has it all. I want to thank Chet Cunningham for handling the story so well. Chet's an ex-infantryman of Korean War vintage, and is the latest addition to my hand-picked corps of professional writers.

Chet has a fine feel for Bolan because, as a screen and fiction writer, he has lived all over the United States, gotten to know the country real well and knows a lot about a lot of different subjects (such as, I happen to know, motorcycles and the Wild West!). But the topicality of his latest subject, the SULCC (Super Ultra Large Crude Carrier), gives a scary punch to his storyline, and I detect here a point of view that aims to *do* something about the critical despoilation of our world's shores. Chet's deep engagement in matters of survival are part of the role he plays in a San Diego writers workshop that has 22 members, 17 of whom are selling novelists.

Mack Bolan's soul continues to be forged, again and again, in the white-hot heat of the hellgrounds, as he moves toward the violent beyond-sanction identity already hinted at in our indispensable Bolan/Phoenix/Able meganovel, *Stony Man Doctrine* (an international bestseller, by the way). Next month, Mack appears in a slave/mobster story that is one of the hardest-edged Mafia books ever written. Watch for it!

Don Pendleton

MACK

THE EXECUTIONER 60

BOLAN

Sold for Slaughter

A federal government agent was missing, a very
special agent. Mack Bolan found her in a chicken
coop in Kansas. At first the sultry beauty did not
recognize Mack. At first she could only moan.

Her name was Smiley Dublin, a Ranger girl from
Bolan's war against the Mafia. She had fallen prey
to pitiless slavers who treated humans like
cattle—abducting, drugging, beating, selling them.

Bolan's gut burned. He'd make the flesh peddlers pay
with their blood. In a Jersey warehouse, he squeezed
Tommy the Weasel till he squealed, then followed a
trail of horror all the way to Algiers.

Which was where the "Bolan Effect" turned a
Garden of Earthly Delights into the fiery pits
itself!

Available wherever paperbacks are sold.

MACK BOLAN
THE EXECUTIONER SERIES

I am not their judge, I am their judgment—I am their executioner.
                                        —Mack Bolan,
                              a.k.a. Col. John Phoenix

Mack Bolan is the free world's leading force in the new Terrorist Wars, defying all terrorists and destroying them piece by piece, using his Vietnam-trained tactics and knowledge of jungle warfare. Bolan's new war is the most exciting series ever to explode into print. You won't want to miss a single word. Start your collection now!

#39 The New War
#40 Double Crossfire
#41 The Violent Streets
#42 The Iranian Hit
#43 Return to Vietnam
#44 Terrorist Summit
#45 Paramilitary Plot
#46 Bloodsport
#47 Renegade Agent
#48 The Libya Connection
#49 Doomsday Disciples

#50 Brothers in Blood
#51 Vulture's Vengeance
#52 Tuscany Terror
#53 The Invisible Assassins
#54 Mountain Rampage
#55 Paradine's Gauntlet
#56 Island Deathtrap
#57 Flesh Wounds
#58 Ambush on Blood River
#59 Crude Kill

Stony Man Doctrine

Available wherever paperbacks are sold.

GOLD EAGLE

Mack Bolan's

PHOENIX FORCE

AN EXECUTIONER SERIES

by Gar Wilson

Phoenix Force is The Executioner's five-man army that blazes through the dirtiest of encounters. Like commandos who fight for the love of battle and the righteous unfolding of the logic of war, Bolan's five hardasses make mincemeat out of their enemies. Catch up on the whole series now!

"Gar Wilson is excellent! Raw action attacks the reader on every page."

—*Don Pendleton*

#1 **Argentine Deadline**
#2 **Guerilla Games**
#3 **Atlantic Scramble**
#4 **Tigers of Justice**

#5 **The Fury Bombs**
#6 **White Hell**
#7 **Dragon's Kill**
#8 **Aswan Hellbox**

GOLD EAGLE

Phoenix Force titles are available wherever paperbacks are sold.

HE'S EXPLOSIVE.
HE'S UNSTOPPABLE.
HE'S MACK BOLAN!

He learned his deadly skills in Vietnam — then put them to use by destroying the Mafia in a blazing one-man war. Now **Mack Bolan** is back to battle new threats to freedom, the enemies of justice and democracy—and he's recruited some high-powered combat teams to help. **Able Team**—Bolan's famous Death Squad, now reborn to tackle urban savagery too vicious for regular law enforcement. And **Phoenix Force**—five extraordinary warriors handpicked by Bolan to fight the dirtiest of anti-terrorist wars around the world.

Fight alongside these three courageous forces for freedom in all-new, pulse-pounding action-adventure novels! Travel to the jungles of South America, the scorching sands of the Sahara and the desolate mountains of Turkey, and feel the pressure and excitement building page after page, with nonstop action that keeps you enthralled until the explosive conclusion! Yes, Mack Bolan and his combat teams are living large...and they'll fight against all odds to protect our way of life!

Now you can have all the new Executioner novels delivered right to your home!

You won't want to miss a single one of these exciting new action-adventures. And you don't have to! Just fill out and mail the coupon following and we'll enter your name in the Executioner home subscription plan. You'll then receive our brand-new action-packed books in the Executioner series every other month, delivered right to your home! You'll get two **Mack Bolan** novels, one **Able Team** and one **Phoenix Force.** No need to worry about sellouts at the bookstore...you'll receive the latest books by mail as soon as they come off the presses. That's four enthralling action novels every other month, featuring all three of the exciting series included in The Executioner library. Mail the card today to start your adventure.

FREE! Mack Bolan bumper sticker.

When we receive your card we'll send your four explosive Executioner novels and, absolutely FREE, a Mack Bolan "Live Large" bumper sticker! This large, colorful bumper sticker will look great on your car, your bulletin board, or anywhere else you want people to know that you like to "Live Large." And you are under no obligation to buy anything—because your first four books come on a 10-day free trial! If you're not thrilled with these four exciting books, just return them to us and you'll owe nothing. The bumper sticker is yours to keep, FREE!

Don't miss a single one of these thrilling novels...mail the card now, while you're thinking about it. And get the Mack Bolan bumper sticker FREE!

BOLAN FIGHTS AGAINST ALL ODDS TO DEFEND FREEDOM.

Mail this coupon today!

Gold Eagle Reader Service, a division of Worldwide Library
In U.S.A.: 2504 W. Southern Avenue, Tempe, Arizona 85282
In Canada: 649 Ontario Street, Stratford, Ontario N5A 6W2

FREE! MACK BOLAN BUMPER STICKER
when you join our home subscription plan.

YES. please send me my first four Executioner novels. and include my FREE
Mack Bolan bumper sticker as a gift. These first four books are mine to examine free for
10 days If I am not entirely satisfied with these books. I will return them within 10 days
and owe nothing. If I decide to keep these novels. I will pay just $1.95 per book (total
$7.80) I will then receive the four new Executioner novels every other month as soon
as they come off the presses. and will be billed the same low price of $7.80 per ship-
ment I understand that each shipment will contain two Mack Bolan novels. one Able
Team and one Phoenix Force There are no shipping and handling or any other hidden
charges. I may cancel this arrangement at any time. and the bumper sticker is mine to
keep as a FREE gift. even if I do not buy any additional books.

NAME   (PLEASE PRINT)

ADDRESS   APT. NO.

CITY   STATE/PROV.   ZIP/POSTAL CODE

Signature   (If under 18. parent or guardian must sign.)

This offer limited to one order per household We reserve the right to exercise discretion in
granting membership If price changes are necessary. you will be notified
Offer expires April 30, 1984   166-BPM-PACR